Ann Summers

Madame B's Stories of Seduction

Ann Summers

Madame B's Stories of Seduction

EBURY
PRESS

1 3 5 7 9 10 8 6 4 2

Published in 2007 by Ebury Press, an imprint of Ebury Publishing

A Random House Group Company

Text written by Siobhan Kelly   Ebury Press 2007

The Random House Group Limited Reg. No. 954009

Addresses for companies within the Random House Group can be found at
www.randomhouse.co.uk

A CIP catalogue record for this book
is available from the British Library

The Random House Group Limited makes every effort to ensure that
the papers used in our books are made from trees that have been
legally sourced from well-managed and credibly certified forests. Our
paper procurement policy can be found on www.randomhouse.co.uk

Typeset by Palimpsest Book Production Limited,
Grangemouth, Stirlingshire

Printed in the UK by CPI Cox & Wyman, Reading, RG1 8EX

ISBN: 9780091916473

CONTENTS

FOREWORD

I'm thrilled and delighted to welcome you to Madame B's *Stories of Seduction*, a red-hot volume of explicit, enthralling true stories told to us by real women. We've hand-picked these tales from hundreds of real erotic confessions told to Madame B. I'm so proud that they celebrate women who do the things you want to do – but would never dare.

There's a world of erotic adventuring for you to enjoy within these pages. I hope you have as much pleasure reading these stories as Madame B did compiling them. I'll let her tell you more.

Jacqueline Gold

Ann Summers, CEO

Dear Reader,

Welcome back to my third volume of bedtime stories that will have you doing anything but sleep! I collect other women's sexual confessions: true stories from women who've lived out their wildest fantasies, and want to share their sizzling secrets with me.

For years, I have written these titillating tales in a red leather notebook that I carry with me everywhere and read whenever I want to lose myself in a steamy story. But the contents of that red leather notebook are so highly charged it seemed a shame not to share them with a wider audience.

Since I published my first two volumes of true confessions, I've been busy gathering new stories to feed the public's appetite for the truth about what women really do. So here is another collection of arousing, astonishing stories from those who've taken their sex lives to the limit and fulfilled their orgasmic potential. Some of their stories are soft and romantic: some are shocking and hardcore. All of them really happened.

Happy reading. And if any of these stories inspire you to have a white-hot, wild adventure of your own and you wish to confess . . . well . . . I'm always listening.

Madame B x

JET

There's something so thrilling about aeroplanes: when you're 33,000 feet in the air, you're neither here nor there. Reality is suspended, and anything goes. There's a very good reason why the Mile High Club has so many members, as this woman found out. Who said air travel was no longer glamorous, exciting and sexy?

You hear about people being upgraded to business class all the time, but you never think it'll happen in reality. Not to ordinary women like me. But it *did* happen to me, and it turned out to be a very memorable journey indeed.

I was flying from Edinburgh to London for a meeting. Any thoughts I might have had about glamorous business travel were dashed when my boss handed me an economy ticket, saying it wasn't worth paying extra for an hour-long domestic flight. When I arrived at the airport early in the morning and handed my passport and confirmation number to the girl behind the desk, her face fell.

'I'm so sorry, but this flight is overbooked,' she said.

She must have registered the mild panic on my own face – I *had* to make this meeting. But before I could even start to plead and protest she tapped away frantically at her keyboard.

'Oh!' her expression brightened. 'Actually, this is your lucky day! We've got a spare seat in first, so we can upgrade you.'

And she handed me a shiny boarding pass and pointed me towards the fast-track security gate. I sashayed through in under a minute, hoping I looked like I belonged in first class. I was glad that the nature of this meeting demanded I wear a suit that day. The security guard who checked my pass directed me to the executive lounge, which was subtly signposted behind a bar. I stepped through a frosted-glass door and into another world. A uniformed bartender squeezing oranges for juice looked up and immediately offered me freshly ground coffee. Free newspapers were strewn across designer glass tables, and on leather sofas that would have looked more at home in a five-star hotel lobby, sat well-dressed, glamorous people passing time before their flights. I looked at them in awe: my new companions all oozed money, power and, of course, sex. And here I was, right among them.

One guy in particular stood out. He was immaculately dressed in a dark-blue pinstripe suit: his jacket fell open to reveal an expensive, turquoise silk lining, and also showed off the flat stomach that lurked beneath his pale blue shirt and tie. His dirty-blond hair was close-cropped, his rugged face and square jaw softened by a pair of pink lips that made a vague pout as he concentrated on his copy of the *Financial Times*. If this was the type of man that flew business class, I was going to have to make sure I earned enough money to do it more regularly.

I was so comfortable that the hour's wait went by quickly and soon my flight to London was called. I was so excited that I was the first one up the stairs on to the jet. As I sank into the burgundy leather chair, easily as big and comfortable as any armchair in my flat, the stewardess handed me a glass of champagne. Yes, I thought, as I kicked off my high-heeled shoes and curled my bare legs up under me, this is the way to travel. It simply does not get any better.

And then I realised that it *did* get a little better. Because who should be sliding his briefcase into the overhead locker than Mr Moneybags himself? The very man I'd just spent an hour checking out in the lounge! Up close, I could see that he was a little older than I'd first thought – around forty, forty-five even – but this only made him look sexier, more distinguished. When he sat down next to me, giving me a formal nod, I could smell his expensive cologne. I also noticed that his nails were manicured and shiny: the man oozed wealth and sophistication in a way that made me feel incredibly aroused.

And I wasn't sure, but I thought that the attraction might even be mutual. I caught him sneak a glance at my bare, brown legs and my pretty toes, painted a flattering shade of pale pink. He thought I couldn't see him behind his copy of the *FT*, but I could. I smiled at him, emboldened by my single glass of champagne, and he immediately broke eye contact and buried himself even deeper in his paper. I wriggled around in my seat, trying to force him to look at me, subtly undoing the top button of my blouse so that when he next looked up, he'd see a tantalising glimpse of the camisole underneath. When I handed my empty glass back to the stewardess before take-off, I made sure that my arm brushed against his.

'So sorry,' I said, even though I was nothing of the sort. I wondered if he, too, had felt a little charge of sexual tension pass between us. I yawned and stretched, showing my waist off to its best advantage and leaned forward so he could see the curve of my breasts. And it started to work: he wasn't concentrating on his newspaper any more and he was starting to look a little bit uncomfortable, as though there was a lot going on beneath that starched Savile Row suit.

The thought of his body, flesh and blood, coming to life underneath that cool, suave exterior, really excited me.

Once we took off, the combination of the jet engine's rumbling, the sheer sensual luxury of the leather seat, and the fact that I'd been writhing and purring like a cat on heat, caused me to become quite aroused. This man was pumping out sexual energy like a power station – and I was absorbing all of it.

I glanced up and met his eyes. Piercing blue and staring right at me, before looking down to my breast. I realised that my hand had been caressing my collarbone and idly tracing the contours of my bosom – I do that sometimes when I'm thinking about sex, but I certainly didn't know I'd started to do it in public. Blushing, I lowered my gaze and when my eyes rested on his lap, there it was – a hard-on . . . with my name on it. His erection looked as big and powerful as the rest of him. A rod of flesh was straining at his trousers, making a little tent of the pinstriped wool. Even as I watched, it grew bigger, and the colour rose in his cheeks as we both silently acknowledged the effect we were having on each other.

He parted his lips and closed his eyes for a moment. I pictured what his face would look like when he came and bam – that mental image, a vivid, horny picture, sent a surge of hot blood to my pussy. A violent throbbing between my legs made me catch my breath. Okay, I thought to myself, you're in trouble now. Initially, I'd been attracted to this guy and wondered what it might be like to fuck him. Now, suddenly, that idle daydream had turned into a physical reality. My problem now was that I *had* to fuck him. No two ways about it. But where? How? And when? Dear God, it needed to be soon. I had never felt this frustrated in my life, and it was making my head spin.

I took a few deep breaths and tried to clear my head. Crossing my legs was something between agony and ecstasy, my throbbing pussy was so engorged that the slightest touch or movement sent fresh waves of tension through my body. What did I do now? We had barely spoken two words to each other. And the 'fasten seatbelt' sign was still on, so even if I wanted to rush to the bathroom to get myself off – tempting, and I knew I could make myself come in seconds – I was stuck in my seat.

As our jet climbed into the clouds, surging through pockets of turbulence, the flipping in my stomach mimicked the adrenaline that was already pumping through my system. Every lurch I felt in the seat stimulated my body further. I closed my eyes, trying to calm myself down, but when I did I couldn't help imagining his body, his chest, his legs. I pictured strong arms, a toned stomach leading to a fuzz of dark-blond hair leading to – oh God, I had to have him. I snapped my eyes open again. He was looking at my tits; glancing down at nipples that had become hard and swollen as I thought about his naked body. His paper was now folded on his lap. Did I dare reach out and touch him? Would I be able to stop once I did?

It was still dark outside and the stewardess dimmed the lights, announcing that we would need to turn on the overhead lights if we wished to continue reading. The tiny electric bulbs above illuminated the cabin like candlelight, bathing us all in a soft, sexy glow. Would he switch on his overhead spotlight and return to his newspaper, or was now the chance I'd been waiting for?

What I saw next made me suck in my breath with delighted astonishment and my hand fluttered automatically to my collarbone, where I began to caress myself again. He undid his trousers and I could tell by the way his hand disappeared under his newspaper that he was stroking himself. He started off with his eyes closed, but then turned to look at me, raising one dark-blond eyebrow. That look was a challenge. And one that I gladly accepted.

I checked no one was looking and then rearranged myself on my large airline chair so that I sat cross-legged, Buddha-style, hitching up my skirt so that it bunched around my middle. First of all, I pulled the gusset of my cotton panties back and forth, enjoying the friction it created on my pussy, grateful at this stage for any stimulation. God, they were soaking: the damp, warm fabric felt like smoothest silk on my hot, wet, aching cunt. Then, turning my whole body towards him so he could see, I pulled my panties to one side. For a while, I just let him look at my pussy, wet and pulsing, my clit dark pink and protruding, aching for his touch but having to make do with mine. He smiled and licked his lips. Then, with my forefinger, I began to fondle myself. I began with gentle caresses to my clit, which sent the first real surge of pleasure to my body. Soon even that wasn't enough, and I slid first one, then two fingers inside myself.

The knowledge that I was showing my sex to a complete stranger, and that we might be caught at any minute – with unthinkable consequences – made my whole body throb with a desire that bordered on fear. Every time I touched myself, it was more heightened, more intense than any caress or stroke I'd ever received before.

He lifted the newspaper to show me his cock. Even in the half-light I could tell that it was big, thick, and the same pale peach colour as his complexion. His smooth hand worked his hard-on, teasing the dark tip of his penis out from under his foreskin. His balls remained encased inside his smart trousers, a small gesture of restraint that I found wildly sexy. I was transfixed as his left hand made smooth, firm strokes along his twitching rod in a steady rhythm up and down, up and down.

My whole body was tingling, from the intense throbbing in my pussy and clit to pins and needles that shot up and down my limbs, turning me to jelly. I was close to climax, and my own teasing of my clitoris became more and more frantic. Perhaps he sensed that I was about to come, because when I was seconds away from the rippling relief of a huge orgasm, he snatched my hand away from between my legs, leaving me wide-eyed and panting, and transferred it to his splendid shaft. When my fingers closed around the warm skin, I heard a soft moan barely audible above the noise of the jet engine. Then, as suddenly as he'd snatched my hand, he threw it off, zipped himself up, looked away from me and moved to get up out of his chair.

But *why*? My mind reeled with resentful confusion whilst my body thrummed with longing. Had I put him off? Had I touched him wrong? I was sure I was going to feel his hands on my clitoris, but maybe I'd misinterpreted him. Disappointment must have shown in my face, because he winked at me and nodded towards the lavatory door. Suddenly I understood, and felt a fresh wave of desire take me as I saw him disappear through the tiny door, his tall, lean body briefly silhouetted against the light inside, his bulk filling the whole area. He was a big man in a small space. We'd have to get very, very close.

I couldn't follow him right away: I waited for the stewardess to attend to someone else, rubbing my pussy the whole time. I couldn't take my hands away. I had never been so wet before, thinking of that craggy face with its soft inviting mouth that I was only seconds from kissing.

Finally the stewardess went to another first-class passenger to refill his coffee. Not even bothering to put my shoes back on, I slipped out of my seat and went over to the toilet door, knocking softly. The door folded to one side, and a strong arm pulled me in. He was there, trousers round his ankles, shirt hanging open with his tie round his neck, a stunning washboard stomach above that beautiful dick; a single vein now pulsed urgently along its length. He pulled me to him and gave me a kiss that was soft and sensitive yet urgent and probing at the same time, pressing his body against mine so that his dick jabbed into my belly. I felt my body melt under his touch, and when he sat down on the loo seat, I gladly let him pull me to him. For a few seconds, we were opposite each other, eyes locked, bodies touching, while he rolled my panties over my hips, down my legs. The cold air of the cabin on the burning skin of my arse, my thighs, my pussy, was exhilarating.

I parted my legs so they were either side of his lap and pulled my skirt up so that he could see my pussy: I wanted him to see how wet and swollen he'd got me. He held his hand flat against my pussy lips, feeling it throb and pulse against his hand. His other hand reached out and softly massaged my tits, making my already erect nipples stand up and darken like pink berries.

I lowered myself on to the trembling tip of his dick, letting the rounded end rest against the entry to my dripping slit for a few seconds. I had meant to hover there, teasing him and me, but I couldn't; I needed him inside me there and then. Not able to wait another second for his dick to fill me up, I lowered myself down, letting his thick, sturdy cock prise apart my lips and open me, penetrate me finally, filling me up, giving me what I needed so badly. I pounded my pussy on to his dick, pushing down with my whole bodyweight, swallowing him up. I wanted to recapture the first thrill of penetration again, so I raised my thighs up until his cock was nearly out of me, then I sunk down again, hard. Every time I bore down on to his hard-on it seemed bigger: I felt fuller, more satisfied, nearer to my orgasm.

My palms were pressed against the walls of the cubicle for balance: legs and arms aching with the sheer effort of holding this position in such a tiny space. For days afterwards, I would have delicious pain in my limbs from the sheer exertion of it all; at the time, I could only think of his face, inches away from mine, and his dick, moving inside me, hot and hard and big and thick. It was the best feeling in the world.

I placed one hand on his shoulder to steady myself, my tense fingers digging into firm, muscular flesh, my other hand on the mirror where it left a sweaty print. I could see my body reflected in the glass, soft flesh a blur of movement.

His hands squeezed and slapped my arse, guided my hips up and down on his dick. My tits were level with his face. Covering his perfect teeth with those amazing lips, he nipped my breasts through my blouse, starting softly and then building up to the more aggressive, urgent stimulation that I needed.

At that moment, a stewardess's voice came over the speaker. 'We will begin our descent in five minutes,' she said. 'The captain has engaged the "fasten seatbelt" sign. Will all passengers please return to their seats and fasten their seatbelts immediately.' We had no more time to enjoy each other's bodies: if we stayed where we were they'd knock on the door and find us in there together, and airlines take a dim view of passengers attempting membership of the Mile High Club. The knowledge that it was now or never just made the whole experience more intense. I writhed on him with my entire body, ground my clitoris into the base of his pubic bone, while he thrust into me so hard that I thought I would explode. I buried my head in his chest, his crisp, masculine scent flooding my senses as I pushed and rubbed against his body, the friction in my clitoris finally spilling over into delicious vibrations that radiated throughout me like concentric circles of pleasure, rippling out from between my legs. I came around his dick, my pussy squeezing and releasing his dick, sucking the life out of it, smelling his spunk and sweat as he pumped me full of hot, white liquid. I shuddered as the waves of pleasure subsided. His heart was pounding but neither of us had time to recover. Suddenly brisk and businesslike, he kissed me again, wiped my pussy clean with a hand towel, pulled my skirt back down over my hips, stroked my hair and then, with a final slap on my arse, he shoved me out, blinking, into the narrow aeroplane corridor.

Walking in a straight line after such an intense fuck was a challenge. By the time I'd slipped on my shoes and checked my make-up again, he was back in the seat next to me. As the lights dimmed for landing, he leaned in and gave me one final, lingering kiss that made me melt inside. It was a kiss goodbye, a final gesture to draw a line under an amazing, once-in-a-lifetime experience. When he left the plane he didn't look back and, as he only carried a briefcase, I didn't see him at the luggage carousel. As I waited in line for a black cab, I saw him speed past in a chauffeur-driven limousine. He didn't see me. There goes the best sex of my life, I thought. And I don't even know his name.

The meeting went well: my in-flight experience had given me a new burst of confidence and I gave a great presentation. That night, in my hotel room, I undressed, exhausted by my day. When I took off my skirt I found his business card in the pocket. Written on the back, with an old-fashioned fountain pen, was his mobile phone number and the details of his return flight to Edinburgh. He had also written, 'Fancy an upgrade?'

I reached for my phone and punched in his number. That's the thing about first class. Once you've experienced it, you can't go back.

MÉNAGE À TROIS

There's a sexual charge to the backstreets of Paris, a smoky, after-dark sensuality that no other city comes close to. Parisians do it better. And as this woman, a famous novelist, told me, they put on a damn good show — even when they don't know they're being watched.

For most people Paris is all about the Eiffel Tower and the Champs-Elysées. But not for me. I've always preferred the sleazy, faded glamour of the backstreets to the slick, polished areas where the tourists go. I love tumbledown apartment blocks, off-the-main-drag cafés and the city's crumbling *fin de siècle* decadence. There's a romance to that kind of bohemian poverty that goes hand in hand with all the things I find sexy: good red wine; ridiculously lacy, scratchy, slutty underwear; men who always carry books around.

But the apartment that I found myself inhabiting in Paris took my love of dilapidated grandeur to its limit. The moment I saw the building, I fell in love with it: a tall nineteenth-century art nouveau building with long windows at which balconies curved up like eyelashes. It was divided into ten different studio apartments. Other people might have minded the stained and peeling wallpaper or the chandeliers with wiring poking out at dangerous angles, but not me. Ever since I was young, I'd wanted to be a writer and live in a Parisian garret, and as my landlady Mme Philippe led me up the clackety wooden stairs to my attic room, I hummed with pleasure that I had finally achieved my dream. As she showed me the room, I loved it immediately. A cast-iron bed dominated it; there was a tarnished Louis XIV mirror that took up the length of the whole wall. An old oak desk leant by the window looking over the twinkling lights of the Latin quarter. This, I decided, would be the perfect place in which to write my new book.

I hung my few clothes in the old armoire, set my laptop up on the desk, checked a few emails and wrote a few notes about my surroundings. A small glass of Merlot would be tonight's only indulgence: I was exhausted from travelling across the UK and France by Eurostar and Metro and needed to sleep. The bed might have been old, and the springs might have creaked when I tossed and turned in the night, but the sheets that Mme Phillipe had provided were pure, white linen, scented with the relaxing aroma of French lavender. I slipped into my favourite negligee and was asleep within seconds, drifting off to the sound of voices from the rooms either side and below and music wafting in from the street.

At about 4 a.m. the strong smell of cigarette smoke woke me briefly. I sat up in bed, my breasts spilling out of my negligee. I wrinkled my nose, thought about getting up to complain but was so tired I fell asleep again almost immediately. The dreams that followed were of smoke trails and mysterious foreign voices making the unmistakeable sound of two people having really, really good sex. I woke up in the morning with a stickiness between my legs and a musky smell on my fingers – I must have been touching myself in my sleep.

I spent the next day exploring my new locale, browsing flea markets and shopping for bread, cheese and wine. I knocked on the doors of the other people in my building; my neighbours were a friendly, artistic crowd, and I met all of them except for those in the room directly beneath mine. None of the people I introduced myself to seemed quite sure who occupied that room. I had lunch in a café, and came home again to write.

That night, I woke again to the acrid smell of cigarette smoke. This time, I wasn't able to go back to sleep quite so easily. I flipped on the lamp next to me and tiptoed out into the hall. Nothing there. But there were voices, a man and a woman's. Back in my bedroom I paced the floor for a while and then I saw it: a thin wisp of grey smoke rising from a tiny crack in the floorboards at the edge of a rug under my bed. There was a hole in the floor. I don't mind cigarette smoke, in fact I think it rather enhances the atmosphere in some bars and cafés, but I do object to having it permeate my clothes and bedlinen. I knelt on the threadbare rug and peeled it back to reveal not only smoke but a chink of light coming through from the room below. Great, that was all I needed. Now without the soundproofing of the carpet, I could hear voices more clearly – a couple murmuring low and urgent. Unable to stem my curiosity, I squashed my face against the crack in the floor and peered into the room below.

What I saw took my breath away. The voices I could hear were indeed a man and a woman beautiful beyond all belief – and they were fucking on a bed ten feet below where I lay crouched on my own wooden floor. It took a while for me to tell where she ended and he began, but despite my initial thoughts of respecting their privacy, I endeavoured to work it out regardless. They both had dark hair and lightly bronzed bodies, both were toned and petite, and together they moved so quickly that the scene looked like a pit of writhing snakes.

As I watched, they pulled apart from their embrace and the woman got on her knees, ready to go down on her lover. Her tidy little arse jutted into the air: her legs were spread to reveal a shock of dark, neatly trimmed, glossy pubic hair, and a sliver of glistening pinky-brown pussy. The man lay on his back, his dick astonishingly large for such a small man. It was darker than the rest of him and bouncy and upright in the way that only young men's dicks are. The noise of her lips sucking on his cock and his moans of ecstasy in response were nearly as exciting as the visual show they were putting on before me. I had gone from mildly annoyed about the smoke to unbelievably aroused by the strangers' lovemaking in about fifteen seconds.

I couldn't help it, I started to touch myself. First of all I circled my nipples through the shot-silk of my negligee, surprised and delighted at how hard they got and how quickly. Dropping the spaghetti straps over my shoulders, I slid first one, then the other breast out and let them trail along the floor, the cold wooden planks arousing my tits more effectively than any lover's caress. I was prostrate now, my arse in the air. Automatically, I slid my hand between my legs and held my palm flat against my pussy. A warm, dry hand against a pulsing, moistening cunt. I slid four fingers inside myself and my grateful hole twitched around them.

The scene on the bed below me developed. He climaxed, pushing his dick further into her face as his own features contorted with pleasure. She pulled her mouth away from him, a thin silver trail of cum and saliva from her lips to the tip of his penis linked the lovers for a few seconds before dispersing. Confident he would return the favour, she sank back into the messy pillows and stretched herself out, lithe and confident as a little cat. Her body was perky and petite like a young girl's but her sophistication and confident demeanour showed that she was very much a woman. She wore dark, dramatic make-up which was only slightly smeared by her lovemaking, and tiny diamonds glittered at her ears. She sighed with pleasure as the man knelt between her legs, forced her knees apart with his hands and went to work, devouring her pussy with the insatiable hunger of a man who hadn't eaten in days. Her facial features softened despite the harsh make-up as she melted under his tongue. She shook and shivered with pleasure, her tiny, triangular tits mesmerising me. The contrast with my own round, pendulous breasts aroused me. I pressed the whole of my body harder against the cold, unyielding floor, gently rocking back and forth, more turned on by what I was seeing and feeling than I had ever been by anything before. As I watched her come, a soft pink blush creeping across her cheeks and chest, warming up that pale olive skin, I quickly held my thumb against my own clitoris. My own orgasm, which arrived in seconds, was as wordless as hers was noisy. Exhausted, I crawled into bed and drifted asleep to the sound of two voices chatting, jazz records playing and occasionally, the odd wisp of smoke. Now that I knew what it signified, I really didn't mind it at all.

I slept fitfully the next night, half waiting for the smell to wake me up. When it did, I was ready. This time I pulled my negligee off straight away so that I could achieve maximum friction between my bare skin and the floor of my apartment. I lay down on the floor, my legs cold and bony on the waxed wooden surface, my top half teased and tickled by the old rug, an empty wine half-bottle to double up as a dildo clutched in my hand. I wanted to know how it felt to have something inside me while I played with my clit. Below me the lovers, unaware of my spying, lay on their sides, lips and legs locked together. When she parted her legs, I could see his dick sliding in and out of her dark little pussy. With my fingers inside me, I fucked the floor, pushing my hips down into my knuckles, using my whole bodyweight to intensify the sensation. The quicker they fucked, the faster I rubbed my clitoris and, at the last minute, penetrated myself with the neck of the bottle, a cold, slippery rod filling me up inside. Again, their own orgasms were so beautiful and powerful to watch that they triggered my own. My pussy gripped the bottle neck in sweet, painful spasms around the cool, solid glass. Only once I'd had my climax, could I experience the deep oblivious slumber that comes after the release of huge tension.

When I rose at noon I expected to see the lovers slumbering in each other's arms, but they weren't there. They never were. They seemed to exist in an intense, passionate little world, existing for each other and only between the hours of midnight and 5 a.m. Who were they? What did they do with the rest of their lives when they weren't making love in this sleazy little room?

That day I wrote thousands of words. It was some of the best work I've ever produced. I'd been struggling with a couple of characters in my novel but after last night's private floorshow and the long and satisfying sleep that followed, they came to life and the words flowed out. The story was becoming a little more highly sexed than my usual style of fiction, but I had been inspired by my midnight lovers. I pounded my laptop late into the night, only leaving my studio for steak and red wine at a little bistro around 11 p.m. When I crept back in, I saw that the light under their door was on.

By then just the smell of those Gitanes was enough to get me horny. At the first wisp of smoke, I was in my usual position. This time the couple lay on their backs with their hands between each other's legs. She had his dick in her fist and was jerking him off fast and furious while he stroked her clit and pussy slowly and tenderly. It was as if they were putting on a performance just for me, but how could they know that they had an audience?

My pubic bone was still bruised from grinding against the floor the night before, so this time I put my pillow between my legs and rocked to a slow, tender orgasm. The irony was that these night-time neighbours were providing me with far more intense and frequent orgasms than any loving or attentive ex-boyfriend ever had. I was having the best sexual relationship to date with a pair of perfect strangers who were unaware of the fact. It was working for me, at least.

The next evening, I didn't even bother going to bed but just waited up for them. I passed the time writing but barely concentrated on my novel as the whole time I listened in anticipation for the door below mine. Every few minutes I inhaled deeply, hoping to catch a whiff of that distinctive smoke, but could only detect my own tuberose perfume. I fell asleep at my desk, awoke at 2 a.m. to the sound of giggles and scuffles and then, only then, when the dry aroma of cigarettes began to seep through the crack in the floorboards, did I know they had arrived.

I peeled back the rug and the two of them were there. They disrobed slowly and revealed their toned, olive flesh inch by tantalising inch. They'd always been naked when I looked at them before, and this slow, deliberate unveiling of their bodies was even more erotic to me than the first glimpse of naked flesh. She wore elegant matching under-wear beneath a scarlet shift dress: he was naked beneath his white shirt and black trousers. I deduced that he was a waiter, but her clothes gave no clue as to her identity - other than a small gold band from her left hand which she removed to place upon the bedside table. He wore no ring . . . ah! These were illicit lovers who hired this room exclusively for their secret, dangerous liaisons.

They made love on the bed this time more tenderly and conservatively than before. He lay on top kissing her tenderly, his tight, toned buttocks and the muscles of his back rippling as he propped himself up on his forearms. I saw the V-shaped muscle at the base of his spine contract with pleasure as he drove his dick inside her, and her sharp heels dug into his calves and her nails clenched his arse as she tried to take him in deeper and deeper. I was on all fours this time, my forefinger frantically pulling at my clitoris, my middle finger probing the entrance to my slit, drawing moisture from my pussy to lubricate the furious rubbing action. I knew their rhythms so well by now I could recognise the signs that she was about to come. When she did so it was with a ladylike sigh but the deep glow on her face betrayed the real passion she felt. As he let out a deep masculine groan I took my clitoris between my thumb and forefinger and gave it a little twist to push myself over the edge into my climax. As I did so, the woman turned her beautiful face up towards mine and made direct eye contact. And as my orgasm caused my legs buckle beneath me and my upper body fall on to the floor with a thud, the expression on her face changed to one of horror. I hadn't thought she could see me through the crack in the floor, but she knew someone was watching her. She knew someone knew her secret. Hurriedly I replaced the carpet, crawled into bed, hoped that she wouldn't knock on the door demanding to know why I had been spying on her.

I wasn't surprised when they never came back and a couple of evenings later, I sealed the hole over with newspaper. Within the week I found my own Parisian waiter who was more than willing to make my ancient bedsprings creak for the remainder of my stay in France. But the memories of their bodies, the sight I'd seen, kept me in sexual fantasies for years – and I believe the erotic inspiration they gave my writing is the reason my last novel sold as well as it did. In fact, I dedicated my book to them, even though I didn't know their names.

THE END OF THE PIER SHOW

What's better than having a gorgeous, charming man absolutely aching with desire for you? Having two guys aching for you, that's what. When her gay best friend Rick fell in love for the first time, Kyra worried that it would drive them apart. She didn't envisage that all three of them would end up closer than ever — almost as close as you can get, in fact.

I love that feeling you have when you walk out into a club or bar or even down the street with a gorgeous guy on your arm: the other girls are jealous, the other guys are intimidated. Whenever Rick and I hit the town together, we turn every head. We look like the perfect couple: I'm blonde while he's dark, I'm slim but curvy, while he's got that classic inverted-triangle build. His tall, good looks and sharp, flamboyant fashion sense, and my long blonde hair and penchant for pelmet miniskirts mean we receive a great deal of envious glances. We are the perfect couple and we both love it. Well, what's the point of a gay best friend if you can't enjoy a little attention when you go out together?

Rick and I have been friends since our first week of college four years ago. My immediate thought when I saw him in his tight, white T-shirt, and jeans that clung to his strong, sculpted thighs, was *who* is that gorgeous man and how do I make him mine? I marched right over and started a conversation with him. Within five minutes it was clear that I wasn't going to be his type. The penny dropped when he asked me if I knew who the 'cute' black guy on the other side of the room was and if he was single. But we had such an instant rapport that I knew we would be firm friends for ever. We shared a flat at university, and while we both had had various boyfriends through the years, the real emotional bond we saved for each other. The joke was that if neither of us met anyone by the time we were thirty-five, we'd have to get married.

Last summer, Rick met someone he finally wanted to get serious about. By that time, I'd moved to London while he was down in Brighton. When I got the call from Rick telling me that there was someone he wanted me to meet, I was instantly intrigued.

'You'll love Sam, Kyra,' gushed Rick. 'He's just amazing; so funny and gorgeous and my God, what a fuck: I'm having the best sex of my life. So when can you come and meet him? What are you doing this weekend?'

I laughed and teased Rick that Sam had better be as good as he made out because never mind any overbearing prospective mother-in-law, meeting *me* was the real test. But joking apart, I had a twinge of jealousy mixed in with my excitement at meeting boy wonder. I cast it to the back of my mind. Of course Sam would be lovely. I'm not losing a gay best friend, I reasoned, but gaining another.

'Prepare a wild time for me,' I said. 'I'll see you on Friday.'

On Friday night I was met at the station by an uncharacteristically nervous Rick, leading a stunningly good looking guy by the hand. Sam had the same tall, Hollywood-hunk body as Rick but he shared my colouring: Nordic good looks with his light tan, dark blond hair and piercing blue eyes.

'It's so good to meet you!' I said. I liked the twinkle in Sam's eye, it told me he would be fun and easy-going, just like Rick.

'You too, Kyra,' said Sam, landing a peck on my check. 'I've heard so much about you.' A trace of stubble brushed against my own soft skin, making me shiver.

'So,' I said, linking one arm with Sam and the other with Rick, as the three of us set off for the bars and clubs of the seafront. 'What wild adventure have you got planned for me this weekend?'

Actually, we didn't have a wild time that evening at all, but a lovely catch-up over dinner at a great little Italian place in The Lanes. We chatted for hours over pizza and a bottle of wine that turned into two, then three, served by a very cute waiter who was decent enough to flirt equally with all three of us. It didn't take long for me to realise that Sam was perfect for Rick: he was attentive, funny and he obviously really cared for my friend.

Plus, the sexual tension between them was hot. Whenever they thought I wasn't looking, they'd steal a kiss and under the table their hands constantly reached for each other. After my umpteenth glass of wine I excused myself and visited the bathroom, when I approached our table on my return Sam was idly stroking Rick's erect nipple. A sudden, vivid image popped into my mind of the two of them fucking, their perfect bodies bathed in sweat and their beautiful, long limbs entangled. It thrilled me unexpectedly and made me shiver with desire: for some reason, when he was up close with Sam, I remembered how sexy I'd found Rick the first time I laid eyes on him. Watching these two together I realised what men saw in girl-on-girl porn. There was something intensely arousing about these two men who were the ultimate in unattainable sex. Well, what woman wouldn't be turned on by the sexual power implicit in turning a gay man straight? And as for *two* of them . . .

I composed myself, tried to ignore the pulse that had begun to beat between my legs, told myself not to be so ridiculous and sat back down at the table helping myself another glass of red wine. You're drunk, I said to myself, shook my head and looked up to grin at my boys.

'Fabulous breasts,' said Sam, making me blush. 'I never really saw the point of tits until I met you, my darling. But now when I look at those puppies sitting up and begging for attention, I'd almost like to play with them.'

Whoa! So maybe I'm not the only one thinking about sex! I mean, Rick and I had always enjoyed exchanging camp, witty banter, but tonight the chat was moving beyond that into definite flirtation.

'Oh no you don't,' countered Rick. 'I've been friends with those tits for years. If they're going to be ineptly groped by any gay man, I think it ought by rights to be me.'

The three of us were giggling madly by this point, but there was something deadly serious about the way Sam looked at me. He really *was* checking my breasts out. To my embarrassment but also my secret delight, I felt my tits harden under my top. I hadn't worn a bra, and my nipples began to poke through my slinky silver vest top. Sam licked his lips, quickly and subtly. Rick watched Sam with a hungry look on his face. I blushed: this sexually charged atmosphere with Rick was brand-new territory. I was turned on, but somehow it felt wrong. Or did it feel right, but I wouldn't allow myself to feel it?

We left the restaurant soon after that, all quite tipsy. On the way home, we had a heated debate about whether the waiter had been checking out me, Sam or Rick. I insisted that a man that good-looking and well dressed couldn't possibly be heterosexual. Rick, on the other hand, insisted the waiter must be straight because he had never seen him out clubbing and he knew every gay man in Brighton.

'. . . because that was a *fabulous* arse – I'd have definitely remembered if I'd seen it before,' said Rick.

'Well,' replied Sam, 'It's possible that he was checking *all* of us out. I mean, we are all three of us outrageously attractive. And anyway,' he went on, rather sobering up now, and with a sly, sidelong glance at Rick, 'Not everyone picks just one type and then sticks with it for life. Some of us can be attracted to boys and girls. Sometimes in the same night.'

Boys and girls? The same night? My mind raced. So was Sam bi? Did my beloved Rick know this? Did he mind? I was completely flustered and confused. And more to the point,' I thought rather selfishly, if he does dig girls, is he attracted to *me*? But even if he was saying he found me attractive, it was probably only in a surface, aesthetic way rather than a sexual one, right? And even *if* he genuinely fancied me, it didn't matter. He was off-limits. He was my best friend's boyfriend and that made him as unattainable as you can get.

I was still musing over this dilemma, hypothetical, of course, when we reached Rick's flat, a lovely little apartment overlooking the sea. Outside, the lights of the pier illuminated the horizon, voices giggled and shrieked, and Friday night was just beginning for many people. But I was tired and more than a little overwhelmed. I made my excuses and went to bed in Rick's spare room.

The boys weren't so quick to go to sleep, though. Through the wall I could hear their low, rumbling voices talking and giggling. Then there was silence and I knew that they were putting their hands on each other's bodies, unleashing the tension that they'd been building up to all night. I could just picture them slowly undressing each other, peeling tight T-shirts and designer jeans off lightly sweating skin to reveal two golden rippling torsos which they would then press together. Their cocks would be slapping against each other in a play fight, their balls against each other's thighs as they kissed urgently, lips and teeth clashing. I replayed this imaginary film of Rick and Sam fucking in my head, my own body growing hot and aroused as I did so. Their muffled noises next door turned to grunts and moans: this live soundtrack made my pussy swell with desire.

Funny, in all the years I'd lived with Rick, I'd never actually heard what he sounded like during sex. We'd always had enough room and privacy to make as much noise as we liked without disturbing each other. But this, this was a new sound, and it was the horniest thing I'd ever heard. The louder the guys got, the more aroused I became until I eventually made myself come. I parted my pussy lips with my fingers, leaving my clit exposed: just ten seconds of light fondling and I came hard, biting down on my lip to suppress my own moans of delight. A warm orgasm radiated waves of pleasure from my clitoris, at last relieving the tension that had been building up all night, since the first time I'd set eyes on Sam.

As my climax subsided and my breathing and pulse rate returned to normal, I padded over to the window and forced it open, letting the warm zephyr blow my hair and bring me back to reality. I got back into bed, enjoying the salty tang of the sea air. I closed my eyes, Rick and Sam were still going at it. As I drifted off to sleep, it occurred to me that perhaps I was *meant* to overhear them. Perhaps they – or at least one of them – wanted it that way.

I awoke at 9 a.m. to the smell of frying bacon. I was touched: Rick had remembered my absolute favourite weekend breakfast – a bacon sandwich on white bread with plenty of ketchup. He burst in without knocking with the sandwich and a glass of orange juice on a tray.

'Breakfast in bed for my lady,' he said, placing the tray on my sheet with a flourish.

'Thanks, honey,' I said, suddenly conscious of my lace nightie, in which my breasts and nipples were clearly visible and, at the sight of Rick in his crisp white trunks, were getting erect again. I tried not to look at his tight pecs, the faintest trace of a lovebite above his left nipple, his strong, broad thighs or his bulging biceps and I especially tried not to sneak a glance at his dick, although the outline of it was clearly visible. This was madness: Rick and I had seen each other in our underwear a million times, but now that I'd heard him fuck, now that I'd rubbed my clit until I came thinking about him and Sam, I felt like I'd crossed an invisible line and that things would never be the same between us. I felt like we'd actually had sex. And most of all, I was convinced that Rick somehow knew all this, that he could read my mind.

But once I'd showered and we'd had a walk along the beach to blow away last night's cobwebs and hangovers, things went back to normality. It was a glorious, hot day and the three of us laughed and joked together but the dark, sexual undercurrent of last night's conversation was absent. By lunchtime, I'd pretty much forgotten about my masturbatory fantasy, although I was reminded again in the afternoon.

I don't know whose idea it was to take a cooling dip – I think it was Sam's. The boys went in first and seeing them waist-deep in the turquoise sea, briny water dripping down their defined torsos, I felt last night's desire return. I decided to join them, reasoning that the cold, refreshing water would calm me down and take the edge off this desire that was threatening to spill over into obsession.

The sea was indeed cold, but it didn't dampen my desire. The boys teased me mercilessly, picking me up and throwing me in the water. The more I squealed, the higher they threw me. They dunked me, picked me up and swung me around. Laughing and breathless, I tried to escape, but I was no match for two such strong men. Sam crept up behind me and pinned my arms behind my back while Rick tickled me, making me writhe and splash as I giggled uncontrollably. Rick knew exactly where I was ticklish – knew that the slightest touch on my sides or my neck were absolute torture. So why was he paying such close attention to the underside of my breasts, my inner thighs and the backs of my legs? He was caressing my hottest erogenous zones, the parts of my body that seemed to have a direct link to my pussy, making it throb and come alive.

As Rick's hands travelled quickly over my body and Sam's chest and cock pressed into my shoulders and the small of my back, the agony of being tickled was replaced by the hot, urgent tension of arousal that has no way of being gratified. My laughter stopped and I broke away from the boys, striking out and swimming strong strokes to take me away from them. I tried to clear my head and work out how to decipher these mixed signals. They seemed pretty serious and I wondered if this was their roundabout way of moving this forward. But how? I was wildly attracted to both guys, but did they want a threesome? Just Sam? Just Rick?

But then it could be that all the flirting, teasing and touching was completely innocent. And if I said something, if I showed I was taking it seriously, it would mean at best having the piss taken for the rest of the weekend, and at worst, I ran the risk of offending the guys, and ruining the best friendship I'd ever had. My mind was no clearer as I turned to swim back to the shore, and seeing Sam and Rick waist deep in the water sharing a slow, lazy kiss didn't help. The sight of Sam's long, pink tongue idly exploring Rick's lips sent a fresh wave of heat between my legs and I couldn't help but wonder if their dicks were hard just below the waves.

Once on the shore, I decided to play it safe. Yes, I was sexually frustrated, but the facts were this: I was a straight woman. These guys were gay. That meant they didn't 'do' women. So I would keep my feelings to myself, enjoy the rest of the evening and either take care of myself with my own right hand or, hopefully, find a straight guy to fuck when we went out tonight.

That Saturday night, Rick and Sam took me to Brighton's most recently opened club. It was under the old arches on the seafront and one look around told me that my chances of pulling a hetero bloke were roughly nil. Inside, it was dark and cavernous with a vast dance floor and lots of little warrens and cubby holes. Green and pink lasers bounced off silver disco balls, and hi-energy dance music was playing at a volume that seemed almost to shake the room. The atmosphere was fun, unpretentious and sexually exciting, even if I wasn't the right gender for these clubbers. We had a couple of drinks at the bar and then the three of us made our way on to the dance floor. As one cheesy disco hit after another kept us dancing, we all grew hot, sweaty and exhausted, three more sizzling bodies in a sea of beautiful people.

I raised my arms above my head as the opening bars of my favourite dance track filled the club: it was a sleazy, suggestive tune with a heavy beat and sexy lyrics. I closed my eyes and let the music take me over, swaying my hips in time with the beat, I rolled back my head so that my long blonde hair trailed over my shoulders.

Before I knew it, Rick was dancing behind me, so close that I felt his belt buckle digging into my back. His arm wrapped itself around my waist, a familiar touch, electrifying now that it was suffused with sexual tension. In front of me, Sam moved closer, his eyes level with Rick's over the top of my head, his hands on my waist, his dick just above the waistband of my skirt. The three of us danced like that for the rest of the song, the guys moving in closer and closer so that by the end of the tune, my swollen, gyrating pussy was wedged in hard between their two thighs and cocks, compressed like a flower between the pages of a book. This had to be deliberate. And if it was teasing, it was cruel; couldn't they see what they were doing to me? My pussy was on fire, every inch of my skin tingled, and frustration and desire must have been etched into my facial features. If this was a joke, it had gone too far.

But then a large, smooth hand on my breast and warm breath on my neck made me realise that it wasn't just a playful joke. Rick and I had always flirted but only ever in the way a gay man and his fag-hag can, totally harmlessly. This was making me wet – there was surely something real in it? Sam cupped my breast, bent his head to my ear and said, 'You know, you're very beautiful. You're enough to turn two gay men straight. For the evening, anyway.'

I didn't need to reply: my nipple hardening between his thumb and forefinger betrayed how thrilled I was. I blinked, speechless, wishing I could see Rick's face to read his expression. Instead, I felt his warm breath on my neck and his voice in my ear. 'Come on, Kyra,' he said. 'You must know what you've been doing to us all weekend?' I whipped my body around 180 degrees to face Rick, unsure of what I would find: I saw him lean in to kiss me and my mind raced a mile a minute. Something was happening now. Would it be weird? The most important friendship in my life was about to change for ever and I didn't know if I wanted it to. What if it was weird? What if it was awful? When the kiss happened, deep yet tender, the stubble on his jaw scraping sexily against my cheek it felt only natural. I wanted more of it. While he kissed me, Sam's hands slid in between my body and Rick's, kneading my tits, finding my braless breasts under the flimsy stuff of my top, caressing them with an expert touch for someone allegedly a stranger to female flesh. As Rick's hard-on pressed into my stomach, I felt the stirring of Sam's cock in the small of my back: two big, hard cocks. The power and desire in me were so overwhelming that I'd have taken my clothes off and fucked the pair of them on that dance floor if they had asked me to.

But they didn't ask me to. Instead, as the song ended,

the three of us momentarily drew apart, all looking at each other in the eye and gasping, half-laughing at our own daring, half-panting with desire. 'You know the best place to take this?' said Sam, grabbing my hand and then Rick's. 'Outside.'

The three of us edged through the sweaty, heaving bodies on the dance floor. By this time I was so turned on that every stranger I brushed against sent a fresh wave of desire pulsing through my body. When we finally emerged into the cold, grey light we didn't discuss where we were going, but instinctively knew we were heading for the pier. Underneath it were a few tumbledown beach huts and nooks and crannies that afforded momentary privacy for lovers who just couldn't wait to get back to their house or hotel room.

The tide had washed the beach clean, and the three of us stood facing each other on the damp, sparkling pebbles, hidden from public view by an upturned boat. Sam was the first to move: he reached out and touched my breast tenderly, respectfully, and so softly that I sighed and threw my head back in ecstasy. He traced a finger from my nipple all the way up my neck, making me shiver with desire and moved in to kiss me. His kiss was rougher than Rick's had been, more urgent and greedy, but his skin was smoother and softer. I struggled to keep my balance as his kisses grew more desperate and probing, and his hands began to pummel and pull my tits, twisting the nipples through my top and making my whole body sing with pleasure and anticipation.

Rick was behind me now, his hands sliding under my top and into the waistband of my skirt, subtly and deftly massaging the top of my arse and the small of my back. I reached behind me and placed my hand on his zipper: even with Sam's tongue in my mouth, I couldn't hide my moan of delight at the size of what was happening in there. My other hand went to Sam's crotch: a bulge of similar girth and hardness awaited me. I began to rub them, slowly at first, then increasing in speed and pressure. The boys' moans told me they liked what I was doing: I fumbled for buckles, trying to unleash both their cocks at once. I couldn't, of course: the feelings rushing through my body were so overwhelming that I could do little else but relax and yield to them.

Sam stopped kissing me for a moment. When I looked into his eyes, they were shining, his beautiful face was flushed and his expression deadly serious. Behind me, Rick reached around to the zipper of my skirt and unfastened it, undid the button at the top with a flick of the wrist. It fell around my feet, leaving me standing there in only my top and a tiny pair of panties. They were next to go as Rick slid his fingers around the waistband, stroked me a couple of times and then gently eased them over my hips, slid them all the way down my legs, his fingers tickling and teasing my inner thighs, the backs of my knees, and finally my ankles. I kicked my panties off, grateful to have the fresh air on my throbbing pussy, and stood there with my legs slightly parted. I lifted my arms over my head for Sam to finish undressing me: he moved forward and peeled my top off over my head, stopping to bite my nipples gently as he did so. I kicked off my summer sandals: I was now naked but for my jewellery, standing on a beach, the cool seaspray and desire making me shiver from head to toe. Every inch of me but my clit had now been caressed and that hardening bud was so hot and yearning that I thought I would die if one of them didn't touch me there, soon, now.

But the guys hadn't finished putting on a show for me yet. Still fully clothed, they leaned towards each other sharing a brief but deep kiss, then undressed each other in front of me. First the T-shirts, which they pulled off each other in practised unison to reveal matching gym-bunny bodies that made me go weak at the knees. Then they kicked off their shoes and finally pulled at each other's belt buckles, expertly undoing them where I had fumbled and failed. As they wriggled out of their jeans, I noticed they wore matching boxers underneath. They stood before me, two men almost exactly alike in size and build, both muscular and lean, but Sam was smooth, blond and his tan was lightly golden whereas Rick's colouring was darker, hairier, more Mediterranean-looking.

I couldn't work out which one of them turned me on more. That's when it hit me: it was not the individual men but the combination of the two that made my clit throb and my pussy ache so. Sam put his hand on Rick's waistband and pulled down the shorts to reveal a big tawny dick, which eagerly bobbed, ready for action. Sam eased his own underwear off and a smoother dick, longer than Rick's but not as broad, winked up at me from beneath a dark-blond bush. Sam went to touch Rick's trembling hard-on, but Rick brushed his lover's hand away.

'Not tonight,' he said, in a voice laden with desire that I hadn't heard him use before. 'Tonight it's not about us. This is about Kyra. This is about pussy.' They took a step towards me. Who would I fuck first? Would they take it in turns? Would they fuck my arse or my pussy? Would they know how to touch my clit, know that I needed their hands, their tongues, right there between my legs?

If our first kisses had been intense, the sensation of our three naked bodies entwined was overwhelming. I began to moan and writhe, I couldn't help myself. Sam kissed me again, my tits rubbing against his smooth chest, his strong arms pulling me close. Together we leaned back against one of the huge poles that supported the pier. Its damp wood splintered in my back but I barely registered the pain.

While Sam kissed me, Rick knelt before me, gently parted my legs and used his fingers to comb through my bush before tenderly parting my pussy lips and exposing my clitoris which quivered, a little pink bud crying out for his touch. He placed the tip of his thumb on it, making my legs shake so violently that I could barely stand. Rick understood, and hooked my legs over his shoulders so that he was supporting my weight and his face was right there between my thighs. I could feel his warm breath on my skin, and slowly he used his tongue to lick his way around my inner thighs, then the edges of my pussy lips, and then he slid his tongue right into the opening of my pussy and whirled it around. Oh God, it felt good. It felt delicious. But there was another, more urgent need in me. My clit was getting harder and hotter, a situation made more intense by Sam's probing, hungry kisses and his hands on my breasts, my sides, my belly. A voice inside my head screamed with frustration: 'Touch my clit, for God's sake touch my clit, put your tongue there, lick it, fuck it.'

As if by telepathy, his tongue was right in there, swirling around my clitoris, darting as nimbly as a little fish, flickering like a candle flame and bringing me to the brink of the orgasm my body had been building up to all weekend.

But Rick broke away just as I could feel the first quivers get ready to rock my body.

'Where did you learn to . . . ?' I said, suddenly suspicious that Rick might have done this before.

'Come on, honey,' he said, with a wink. 'I didn't just read your glossy mags for the fashion. Those sex pages tell you all you need to know!'

That broke the ice and then the three of us collapsed in laughter and desire. We all lay on our backs, watching the coloured lights above flash through the slats in the pier. I had a cock in each hand: Sam idly stroked my clitoris, keeping up just enough pressure to keep me simmering on the edge of an orgasm but, tantalisingly, not enough to bring me to one.

'I never knew breasts could be so horny,' said Sam, leaning over to take my nipple into his mouth and suckle it gently. Rick followed his lead so that I had a man on each breast and a cock in each hand.

'I need to get inside you,' said Rick, whipping his mouth away from my breasts with a tiny nip that made my whole body arch. From the pocket of his jeans he pulled out a condom: he tore the wrapper open and I watched in fascination as Sam smoothed the sheath down over Rick's erection.

Gratefully, I spread my legs and let him penetrate me.

'Oh God,' sighed Rick as his big, hard dick slid into

my yearning pussy: a broad, sturdy hard-on that was as big as I could handle, and then, as he shifted his body-weight on to me, a little bigger still.

'Oh God,' he mumbled. 'It's so soft and warm in here. I never knew a cunt could feel like this.'

I hooked my ankles around his arse, pulling him deeper and deeper into me. Beside us, Sam knelt with his dick in his hand, stroking it, concentrating on the tip. A fat drop of pre-cum liquid glistened in the moon-light. His eyes devoured my tits and Rick's arse. You could tell it was the horniest thing he'd seen in a long time. Rick's kisses and his cock inside me were doing the job and I knew I that all it would take for me to come harder than I ever had before would be the tiniest pressure on my clit.

Sam tapped Rick on the shoulder and as if by prior agreement, Rick pulled out of me. After gazing at my swollen pink pussy for the time it took him to put on a condom, Sam was suddenly inside me, his dick rocking backwards and forwards, his pubic bone grinding deli-ciously into my yearning, frustrated clitoris. My whole pussy began to flutter like a butterfly, always a sign I was mere seconds away from orgasm. And, I could tell by the look on his face, so was he. He arched his back and closed his eyes, preparing to surrender to his climax. As he did so, Rick straddled me, removed the condom and stuck his naked cock in Sam's mouth. Sam sucked greedily on Rick's big erection, the noise of his lips on his lover's dick was obscured by the crash of the waves.

Rick came first: I saw his balls twitch and rise up into his body and his butt cheeks tense as his orgasm took hold. He made an incredibly intimate noise, a long, guttural growl, and a dribble of spunk from his cock splashed out of Sam's mouth and on to my tits. Sam began to massage the warm, white liquid into my skin, teasing my breasts for the last time and then finally he placed one forefinger against my clitoris, drew back his hips and then pounded, hard. I let myself go. My whole body shook, my clitoris hummed, letting the waves of pleasure wash over me again, again, again and again. As my pussy contracted and squeezed around Sam's dick, he too tripped over into an intense climax, his beautiful, fair features going blank while he abandoned himself to the sheer pleasure of it all.

The three of us lay entangled, breathless and elated, watching the first pink sunrays of dawn over the water. We didn't move even when the cold tide came and washed our bodies clean. Instead, we clung to each other for warmth.

'So,' I said. 'Have I turned you?'

'I never thought I'd do that with you,' said Rick. 'But I'm so glad that I read those magazines!'

'I think we can save this for a weekend treat,' said Sam. 'Will you come again?'

'Oh,' I said. 'I'll come again. And I'll come, and come, and come!'

I HEARD LOVE
IS BLIND

We've often been told 'Look, don't touch.' But what happens when that turns to 'touch, don't look?' A sensory sexual experience you'll never forget . . .

Girls who look like me don't often get to fuck boys who look like Jamie. He's the kind of man who walks down the street in old clothes with unwashed hair and has women falling at his feet. The first time I saw him, it was like a slap in the face – actually, a slap in the pussy, because I felt my stomach lurch and then all the blood in my body rushed to my pelvis. I saw him in a bar and had to talk to him; I walked right over and asked him if he was a model. Of course, he was. Up close he was even more beautiful than from a distance: jet-black hair with a subtle curl in it, olive skin and green eyes, a fine aquiline nose and a lean, athletic body to die for. He's nineteen, half-Indian, half-Irish and fully divine as far as I'm concerned. Since I met Jamie, I *always* want to do it with the lights on.

And then there's me. Seven years older than him, about a hundred grand a year richer, and yes, my IQ is probably a little higher than my beautiful boy's. He is as entranced by my conversation as I am by his body. The first time I took him to bed, he showed himself to be a tender and eager, if a little inexperienced, lover. He is certainly no longer inexperienced: I've taught that boy every trick and technique in the book. He's been a very eager pupil.

There's only one real problem with Jamie, and that's the way he worries that I only love him for his looks. He thinks he's just a trophy boyfriend: a hot young stud on my arm. I tell him that's not true; it's as much to do with his big, thick dick and his firm pink tongue as with those razor-sharp cheekbones or his taut six-pack.

'I've had people judge me on my looks my whole life,' he said. 'I want you to love me for myself as well as my body.'

Of course I tried to reassure Jamie that the way I felt about him wasn't just skin-deep. But on a certain level, I was a bit worried that it was true. I got more aroused from watching him than I did by his touch. I once read that women aren't aroused by visual images, that we need the whole package: romance, candles, hours of sensual massage. Whoever wrote that bullshit had obviously never seen Jamie naked with a hard-on jutting out from between his lean, rippled thighs.

But one night, Jamie decided to test me. The pupil became the teacher for the night; and it was one I'll never forget. It was late November and it was cold outside. I'd laid a real fire in my apartment, partly to create a sensual atmosphere and partly to encourage Jamie to take off his clothes. I'd just bought a new leather sofa and I wanted to fuck him on it, his light brown skin sticking to the smooth leather, his body bathed in the glow of the fire-light. I'd been picturing the scene in my head for days and it had me horny as hell.

Right on time at 8 p.m., Jamie knocked on the door with a cheeky smile. He carried a dark blue paper bag in one hand and a bottle of Moët in the other.

'This is for you, darling,' he said, kissing me on the cheek and handing me the cold champagne. 'And so is this,' he continued, waving the bag under my nose. 'But I'll save it for later.' He had a cheeky smile on his face that I couldn't quite read.

Intrigued, I helped him out of his coat; underneath he was wearing shapeless, baggy jeans and an old sweater. As he disappeared into the kitchen to pour the champagne, I chucked another log on the fire, hoping he'd remove a layer or two of clothing.

We drank our wine and spent some time indulging in lazy kisses on the sofa. Every now and then, I'd stop just to gaze at his gorgeous face. Jamie unfastened the buttons of my shirt-dress one by one, rolled my hold-up stockings down the length of my leg before pulling them off, lavishing on my body slow, sensual kisses as he went. Ever the tease, he kept his own clothes firmly on. My skin began to tingle in anticipation of him taking those layers off. The first time I caught a glimpse of Jamie's flesh was always thrilling. The sight of his torso, his stomach, his arse, always marked the moment between arousal and desperation, triggered a need to have him there and then. He knew this, of course: the longer he waited before getting naked, the wetter I would finally be when he did.

Lovingly, he unhooked my bra and then slid the straps over my shoulders, pulling the cups down to reveal my breasts. He took a nipple between his soft lips, rolled his tongue and used it to flick my nipple gently before sucking. He bit my panties and used his teeth to pull them off my hips and down over my legs, his tongue and teeth teasing my skin all the way down. It was delicious: if only he'd undress, it would be perfect. Maybe he wants me to beg, I thought. And I wasn't too proud to do that.

'Baby,' I purred, writhing on my leather couch, sticking my tits out and spreading my legs, 'Let me see you. *Please.* You know how turned on I get when I can see you.'

What Jamie did next happened so suddenly I didn't have time to react. He leapt on to the furniture, straddled me and, pulling my arms above my head, used my own stockings to tie me to the chrome arm of the sofa. I was pinned down by the bondage and the weight of his body across my chest. Adrenaline coursed through my veins, and a pulse between my legs started to beat as fast as my fluttering heart. The last thing I saw was Jamie reaching over to the blue paper bag he'd brought with him and pulling out an eye mask. He held it up so I could see it, red, padded silk with a black lining, before fastening it tight around my head. I couldn't see a damn thing. And I was still too shocked to speak.

Robbed of my sight, I immediately felt an increasing awareness of all my other senses. I was aware of the soft denim of Jamie's jeans on my belly where he was straddling me, the weight of his solid body pressed into mine, and then, as Jamie leaned his face down towards mine, of his warm breath on my breast, collarbone, near my ear.

'You're so hung up on what you can see,' he whispered, in a low rasp that made me shiver, 'That you've forgotten how horny your other senses can be. I'm going to take you on a sensory journey tonight that will blow your mind and have your pussy begging for mercy.'

Although his words aroused me, I was angry with Jamie, too. How dare he deprive me of my favourite part of making love to him? I opened my mouth to tell him off as he leapt off my body and used my other stocking to bind my feet to the other end of the sofa.

'Let me go! Jamie, what the fuck?' I shouted.

'No,' he replied. As I struggled, I felt a heightened awareness of my body. I felt the dampness beginning to form between my glowing skin and the leather of the sofa. My hair trailed over my shoulders, caressing my décolleté. I was intensely aware of the warmth of Jamie's body, the searing heat he radiated. Jamie's scent, the sexy smell of his hair, carried over in the warm air and I inhaled it like it was a drug, an aphrodisiac.

He disappeared to the kitchen. I tried to break free, thrashed my head about in an attempt to dislodge the blindfold but the more I struggled, the tighter my bonds became. And the more helpless I felt, the more aroused I grew. Every inch of my skin was on red alert, waiting to respond to Jamie's touch. I heard clinking noises from the kitchen, the sound of the refrigerator opening and closing. What was he doing in there?

I soon found out when he returned. 'Your first sensory experience,' he announced, 'Is taste and smell.' I felt his warm, masculine presence as he knelt down next to me and smelled the sharp, sugary tang of fresh fruit. Jamie placed a strawberry between my lips and it tasted exotic and exciting, as though I'd never eaten one before. My lips closed around the succulent fruit as Jamie placed another strawberry on my wet pussy lips, inserted the fruit a little way into my slit. It felt like the tip of Jamie's dick when he was prising me open, preparing to thrust into me. The teasing, ticklish presence of a strawberry was sweet agony, only serving to remind me just how much I wanted him inside me.

He twisted the red berry to and fro, rotating it in my opening, then whipped it away from my pussy and passed it under my nose. I could smell my own personal fragrance as well as the cloying sweet smell of the fruit.

'This is how you smell and taste,' he said. 'Your pussy is sweeter than any fruit.'

I heard him eat the fruit and pictured the dark pink juices staining his soft lips. When he bent down to kiss me, I could taste myself and the fruit, and also something earthy, something basic, an indescribable taste that was the essence of Jamie himself. Our kisses grew more urgent as he lay on top of me, and the sounds of zippers and fumbling denim told me that finally Jamie was going to get naked, like me. If I couldn't see him, feeling his body on mine would be the next best thing. I felt soft cotton brush my face as he lifted his T-shirt over his head and I felt lean hips press into mine as he wriggled out of his jeans. He was naked now, his body skimming mine, his expanding dick lying against my thigh.

'I wish I could see you,' I wailed, frustrated.

'But you always look at me. This is the only way I get to look at *you*. I'm looking at you now,' he said, his voice low and punctuated by deep breaths. 'Your long legs, which you spread for me. I adore the freckles you have on your collarbone. Your tits, which I love so much.' As Jamie described each erogenous zone, my skin sang with pleasure as though he were touching me with hands, not words. Beneath my blindfold, the world was black, but Jamie's descriptions were so detailed that, for the first time, I thought about my body, not his, and it was the sexiest thing ever. 'Your tits are just the right size, I can fit one in each hand,' he said, and put his hands over my breasts. I sighed with pleasure. 'I love the fact that your nipples are pink, they're not brown like mine are.' He continued talking in that sexy, rumbling voice, trailing a hand down my breasts, over my belly, past my bush and finally using a thumb and forefinger to part my pussy lips and expose my clit. 'I love the fact that you're pink down here, too. I adore the way you shave your whole pussy, so that I can see the skin below. I love the shape of your cunt, your soft labia, and I love your clit. It's so tiny, and pretty. Best of all I love to lick it, and rub it, and play with it until I make you come. And when you do come, I love what happens to your face. You go all pink and pretty, and you look so soft and sweet.'

There was the sound of more rustling as Jamie pulled something else from the dark blue paper bag which had contained the blindfold. I heard a click and then a whir, the unmistakable sound of a vibrator being switched on. My clit throbbed in anticipation: before I met Jamie, I was addicted to my vibe, but I hadn't used it since I met him. As he placed the soft, buzzing rubber against my nipples, I realised how much I'd missed using sex toys; I guess that Jamie had become my plaything. I felt my nipples respond to the vibrations, growing harder and bigger until the stimulation was almost too intense and I begged Jamie to stop.

'Oh, I wish you could see your tits now,' he said, 'Your nipples are dark pink and swollen. They look like rosebuds, they're beautiful . . .' and then his soft wet mouth was on my breast, his tongue and lips soothing the tingling skin.

He worked his way down the length of my body with the vibrator, swirling it around on my inner arms, my belly, before holding it still on my inner thighs where it was close enough to my clit to make it thrum and throb but not close enough to give me the intense stimulation I needed to bring me off. He ran the vibe along my pussy lips, probing my slit with the tip of the toy, slowly inserting it so that I cried out with pleasure. He removed it equally slowly, parted my thighs a little further and placed the vibe against my arsehole. I'd never been touched there before, not even by my beautiful Jamie, let alone with a vibe, and the feeling was so intense I let out a strange, animalistic yowl of desire.

'I think you're ready for me,' announced Jamie and, leaving the vibe buzzing against my arse, he speared me with his dick. Every hair on his rich, luxuriant bush tickled and teased the bare skin on my own pudenda, the base of his cock finally gave my clit the friction I'd been craving all along. I could smell my pussy juices mingling with his own primal aroma, everything heightened in my blindfolded state. He pounded away, each thrust intensified by the vibe probing and teasing my arse, and I felt the first unmistakable pre-orgasmic contractions ripple through my body. It was going to be huge, I thought: the strongest, most amazing orgasm I'd ever had. I let my flesh go limp in anticipation of my climax but Jamie stopped suddenly.

'I'm going to untie you now,' he said. 'But only if you promise to keep the blindfold on.' I nodded my assent; I was so desperate for an orgasm I'd have agreed to keep the blindfold on for the rest of my life if he would only allow me to come in the next few minutes. Jamie tugged at the stockings that bound me to the sofa, more urgently than when he'd tied me up, obviously as eager as I was to resume fucking, to chase that climax. The blood pumped back into my newly freed hands and feet, sending a tingling numbness along my limbs. Jamie placed his hands around my waist – why had I never noticed how large his hands were, how dry and papery and soft they felt against my skin? He flipped my yearning body over so that I was on all fours.

With his hairy knee back between my smooth thighs again, he parted my legs, used his fingers to find my hole, pulled apart my quivering cunt before poking it with the tip of his dick. He was inside me then; he fucked me eagerly from behind, one hand on my hips to steady me, his smooth long dick probing the entire length of my dripping pussy. With his free hand, he placed the vibe directly on my clitoris and I knew I couldn't hold out much longer. The limbs that had been numb now flooded with feeling as the tension crept up and then erupted as I came. My pussy contracted and released in four or five hot, intense waves, my cunt clutching at Jamie's dick. I remained blindfolded and crouched on all fours as tiny spasms gripped my pelvis, the aftershock of my climax. Jamie whipped his dick out and came into the air, his warm, white liquid raining down on my arse.

He used strong, flat hands to massage his juice into the small of my back. A tiny dribble ran down the crack between my buttcheeks: Jamie followed it with his thumb, making tiny circles and rubbing his spunk into the opening of my arsehole, a sensation that left my breathless.

As I lay there in the darkness, it occurred to me that I'd been so turned on by the way Jamie tasted, smelt, sounded and felt, that I hadn't thought about what he looked like the whole time we'd been fucking. I felt a new respect for my beautiful lover, who had proved with his passion and imagination that he was more, so much more, than a pretty face. I felt tender, deft fingers untying the blindfold that I had been wearing. I realised it had grown dark outside while we were fucking. I blinked for a few seconds, my eyes adapting to the soft light that came from the dying embers of the fire. When I rolled over to face Jamie, I could only vaguely make out the contours of his body, silhouetted by the glow. The details of his physique that drove me crazy – the line of hair between his navel and his dick, the colour of his nipples, the veins on his arms, the dimple on his left cheek – none of these were visible. I didn't mind a bit.

'Want me to put the light on, baby?' he asked as he ran a finger from my breast to my thigh. I could barely see him, but to me he had never looked so beautiful.

RUMBLE IN THE JUNGLE

One of the most persistent sex myths is that a hot fuck needs to be with someone you love – or at the very least, like. Sometimes, a little tension and antagonism between two people can fan the flames of a fire that burns hotter than any romantic flame. Hell, I've had some of the best sex of my life with people I couldn't stand. The woman who told me this tale took an instant dislike to the man who was to become her most passionate lover. I love this story: it proves the point that uncontrollable desire manifests itself in the most unlikely places, and is often inspired by the strangest people.

I looked around the walls of my mud hut, on a nature reserve in the middle of the Indian jungle and thought to myself: how did I end up here? When my friend Sarah suggested a holiday with a difference, I jumped at the chance to do something other than the usual sunloungers-and-cocktails shtick. In the brochure, this health-kick holiday in the wild had seemed like a great idea: yoga every morning, herbal tea, vegetarian food and long-distance hikes through lush countryside. I had visions of emerging as a thin, spiritual creature, unburdened by Western ideas of beauty and values. I had looked forward to traditional Indian beauty treatments to leave my skin glowing, and returning to the UK tanned, blissed-out, serene. And of course I had hopes of making an amazing sexual connection with some bronzed, toned, dreadlocked gap-year student who would make soft, tender love to me on the shores of the Arabian sea. Well, what's the point of being a single girl on holiday if you don't enjoy every facet of your freedom?

All those visions were cruelly shattered when Sarah cancelled on me at the last minute because of a work assignment she simply couldn't get out of. I toyed with the idea of staying at home, but I'd paid for this trip, so I travelled alone, still buoyed by a sense of adventure and anticipation. The reality of it was, I was sleeping under a smelly mosquito net in a crude mud hut, surrounded by ageing hippies who routinely tried to outdo each other with extreme travel stories.

'Of course, this is just a mild weekend,' said a bare-footed guy with a straggly grey beard and a sagging pot belly. 'The real hardcore ones are the kind where you go to an ashram and live off only juice. You get a really clear head after the first few days. It's very spiritual.'

The only person my age was David, and frankly he was even worse than the old hippies. An outward-bound instructor from the West Country, he was convinced he knew everything about anything and his arrogance pissed me off from day one. He also thought he had a great body, which he insisted on displaying at every possible opportunity – we couldn't pass a waterfall without David suggesting an impromptu group shower. I suppose that he *was* good-looking, if tall, ripped, muscled guys without an inch of fat and strong, smooth brown bodies are your thing. And if you go for strong jaws, melting, hazel eyes and soft waves of light brown hair, well, David might be your type. However, he could have looked like Brad Pitt but his awful, know-it-all, patronising personality would have turned my stomach.

Of course, as I was the only single woman under forty there, David made a beeline for me. He didn't understand my reluctance to sit around the campfire every night listening to him bang on about mountains he'd climbed and rapids he'd ridden. I started off by giving him the polite cold shoulder but after day two I was openly snapping at him. Mild irritation turned to a slimy, creeped-out feeling that I couldn't shake. Every night as I settled down to sleep, I cursed Sarah for leaving me alone with these people in the middle of nowhere. I found David so intensely annoying that he was the last thing I thought about before I slept. And when he crept into my dreams, my explicit erotic dreams that made me wake bathed in sweat, throbbing between the legs and clutching the bedclothes, well, I just took it as a sign that he was such an irritating arsehole that he could even creep into my sleep uninvited.

Towards the end of the week, I was having fun despite myself. I loved the daily yoga sessions – all five hours of them. And I also enjoyed what was happening to my body: cellulite was turning to firm, toned flesh and inches were melting off me. I had to admit that I was regaining my teenage figure, and with it a renewed appetite for sex and love. I suppose the daily sixteen hours of blazing sunshine and steamy atmosphere made it a bit of a sexy place, too. It was just a crying shame there was no one to get horizontal with apart from David, and he obviously didn't count.

Halfway through the retreat I was starting to get to grips with the advanced yoga sessions. I had become something of an expert in recent days. Call me shallow, but while all the hippies were omming and breathing through alternate nostrils, I was thinking things like, 'Now that I can do the splits, there's loads of sex positions I can try out that I wouldn't have dared attempt before.'

David showed off by doing a headstand, a feat made less impressive by the fact that he would always look around afterwards to see if I was watching him and how manly he looked. What did he expect me to say to him? 'Well done for having such strong legs. Now, let's fuck.' maybe he did. Well, I wasn't going to give him the satisfaction.

The weird thing was, the more I grew to despise David, the hotter my dreams were. The fact that he had edged into my sexual fantasies made me more short-tempered with him than ever. After I'd snapped at him for invading my space during evening yoga, I heard him mutter something about me just needing a damn good fuck, but when I asked him to repeat himself, he denied having spoken.

On the Thursday morning, the second-to-last before leaving, we performed our sun salutations as the dawn broke over the Indian jungle. This was probably my favourite part of the day, feeling the first rays of sunshine kiss my skin in my bikini. Deepa, our yoga instructor, told us that today we would be doing assisted stretches with partners.

'This works best with one man and one woman,' she said. 'I've allocated partners depending on your strength and size.' I knew it, I *bloody* knew it, even before she read out my name with David's.

'Well,' he said, lecherously, striding towards me with his yoga mat underneath his arm. 'Deepa is obviously keen for us to get to know each other a little better.'

'Well I'm not,' I snapped. As we lay next to each other on the floor and did the deep-breathing exercises that were supposed to give an increased awareness of our bodies, I found that all I was getting was an increased awareness of David's. As I concentrated on breathing slowly in through my nose and out through my mouth, I felt a tingling pass through my body that I hadn't experienced doing yoga before. A heat that started between my legs and grew with every breath, a sensation like the plucking of a string somewhere deep in my pelvis, and I realised with dismay that as much as I hated David, lying next to him like this was turning me on. *Really* turning me on.

Now that I was close enough to his body to smell him, now that the tiny hairs on our arms were brushing against each other, I realised that I was close to the place where the body decides to override the mind. When chemistry strikes, there's nothing you can do about it. Even if you don't like his personality or his looks even, your body's reactions tell you that when your skin touches his for the first time, you're going to receive an electric shock, a surge of adrenaline and lust so powerful that you're simply going to have to kiss him and once you start you won't be able to stop and it will escalate into the kind of hot, sweaty, steamy sex that will wake you up in the night and make your stomach flip whenever you think about it for the rest of your life.

I'd known great sexual chemistry before with one or two lovers. But they had been men I liked, respected, sometimes loved. This utter contradiction of body and mind was new to me, and very unsettling.

The rest of the partnered stretching session was a sweet kind of agony. David and I had to hold a variety of intimate poses. It was fine to start with, when we sat back-to-back, taking it in turns to lean on each other. His body was so honed that I could feel the large sinews of his back rippling against my own flesh. But as long as we weren't facing each other, I could control the animal urges that ripped through me, ignore the fact that the hairs on my neck stood on end and that the sensation between my legs was growing more, not less, intense.

I even had things under control when we raised each other's arms above our heads and pushed against them, using the resistance of the partner's body to increase our muscle strength and stamina. As we worked our way through a variety of poses, none as intimate as I'd at first feared, I began to master the art of mind over matter. By breathing deeply and concentrating on how *my* body felt rather than David's (just out of interest it was warm, damp with fresh perspiration, young, virile and firm), I could calm myself down. Yes, I'd experienced a huge rush of arousal when we were lying next to each other. But it was okay now. I was calmer now. And if I still felt a little shiver whenever we changed position and a new patch of his skin made first contact with an exposed area of my own, well, that was probably just sunburn.

Deepa told us to change positions again. I had to sit with my legs as far apart as I could get them while he used pressure on my inner thighs to push them a little bit further apart, stretching my body as far as it could go to test it and further increase my flexibility. David's palms touched the sensitive, thin skin between my legs, always a favourite erogenous zone. My pussy began to pump and throb in earnest, a horny little heartbeat between my thighs. To my acute shame, a damp patch appeared on my bikini bottoms, my body refusing to listen to my mind yet again. When David noticed this, the smug, self-satisfied way he licked his lips should have turned me off but instead the glimpse of his tongue made me realise how easy and delicious it would be to lean forward a couple of inches, slide the tip of my tongue into his mouth and let the kiss happen, to set the whole chain of events in motion.

Before I could do anything so foolish, our yoga lesson

drew to a close and it was time to change into walking gear for our jungle trek. I stormed off to my hut, shut the door behind me and kicked the bed in annoyance and frustration. Fuck fuck fuck fuck *fuck*! Sleeping with David was out of the question. Sure, I was horny. Sure, I got wet every time I even thought about what we'd be like together. But I wouldn't give that smug bastard the satisfaction.

That day's walk took us up a steep overgrown path. We were to hack our way through the rainforest to the summit of a mountain where we would have our packed lunches (vegan, low-calorie of course) by the top of a mountain before planning our descent. It was the hardest hike we'd done yet, but I strode ahead of the pack, the vigorous exercise helping to displace the morning's unwelcome burst of desire. Eventually I fell into step with the rest of the group and almost forgot about David and the way he'd looked at me when he'd seen the expanding damp patch on my crotch.

More than once I found myself walking close to him but when this happened I'd stride on and strike up a loud conversation with one of the other trekkers, sticking to narrow bits of the path so he couldn't tag along. But I couldn't shake him off. When he was behind me I felt him checking out my arse in my little shorts, his eyes boring into me. And when he was in front of me, I couldn't help my own eyes being drawn to his impressive back. Couldn't help but be transfixed by those two slabs of muscle on top of the most strong, flexed, manly thighs I'd ever had the pleasure of ogling. Sometimes I'd look at his hands swinging by his side, helping to keep his balance. Even his wrists made me horny. The nape of his neck, sinewy and deeply tanned, oh God, I wanted to reach out and touch it.

Looking back now, I wonder if David knew that I was hypnotised by his body. Because I was staring at it so intently that I didn't realise until I turned to speak to the woman next to me that we had broken away from the group. I looked around in a panic and saw no one. I listened for the murmured conversation that would guide us back to our companions, but it was such a steep climb everyone would be too out of breath to talk. When he heard my footsteps stop, David turned around, a smirk playing on his lips.

'I thought you were supposed to have outward bound skills!' I panted at him. 'Can't you get us back to the rest of the group?'

'Oh dear,' he said, in a voice laden with sarcasm. 'I didn't realise you were following me so closely. Looks like it's just the two of us. Whatever are we going to do?'

Why, *why* did he have to look so fucking horny when he was being so obnoxious? Rather than his arrogance diminishing his sex appeal, the way I felt about him actually seemed to add to it. Exhausted, I sat down on a tree stump.

David slid his backpack off, reached into it and pulled out his water bottle. 'Whatever are we going to do?' he repeated, before tilting his head back and drinking greedily, letting the water spill out of his mouth and splash down his well-defined brown neck. My body was telling me to throw myself at him, lick up the cascading water, to rip his clothes off his body and keep kissing, licking, sucking and biting until I got to his cock . . . and when I got there, to keep going until he was hard, harder than he'd ever been in his life, finally hard enough to fuck me the way I wanted him too.

'You ought to drink something,' said David, in that annoying know-it-all voice. I realised that I was absolutely parched. I also realised that I had drained the contents of my water bottle before we were even halfway through the hike. I shrugged my shoulders as if I didn't care, but too late, he'd spotted the empty bottle dangling from my belt.

'Have some of mine,' he said. And he placed the neck of the bottle next to my lips. I drank greedily, partly from thirst and partly because I could taste David on the bottle. It smelt of him, and I closed my eyes, pressing the bottle to my mouth, imagining it was his kiss. When I took my last swig, the water cascaded down my chin, cheeks and neck.

I was frozen to the spot as David bent down and extended a clean, pink tongue and caught a dribble of water running down my neck. His tongue touched first my collarbone, then swept up my cheek tantalisingly slowly. He was so close I could feel each hair on his neck, breathe in that hypnotic scent of his. His tongue reached my lips and gently prised them open, followed by a pair of smooth, soft lips that were so much the right shape, size and texture that they could have been designed expressly for the purpose of kissing mine. I couldn't have resisted even if I'd still wanted to.

This was no longer a question of wanting David: I needed him. It was a primal urge, like hunger, like pain, like sleep. I *needed* to have his hands on my tits, so I pulled open my cotton shirt, not caring as buttons scattered into the undergrowth, lost for ever. He obviously needed it too, because he unhooked my bra with the same expertise he did everything else and placed hands that were twice the size of my breasts and covered them. My nipples grew hard under his warm touch and poked out through his thumb and finger. He squeezed them gently, a soft, tender touch that made my clit throb with anticipation.

I wanted him to undress me fast, quick, urgent; any

scrap of material between us was a hindrance, holding up the moment I could feel his chest pressed against my tits, his hands on my arse, his cock in my cunt. I tore at his shirt. My hands turned to claws, I was a wild animal as I yanked off his belt and pulled his trousers and pants over his hips while he removed my own shorts. My clothes were around my knees when he parted my inner thighs again and jabbed two fingers inside my dripping pussy. I could feel my greedy hole contract around them and he took them out all too soon. He held those two fingers up like someone miming a pistol, and ran his hand underneath his nose, breathing deeply.

'You're soaking,' he said. 'And, fuck me, you smell delicious.'

A fat dick bounced between his thighs: he was clearly so eager to fuck me, I didn't need to use my mouth to make him any harder. I reached both hands down, tugged at the shaft of his penis, began at the base and caressed the length of him before finishing with a swirl and a flourish, peeling his foreskin back to reveal a glistening, purple tip. It was the best-looking dick I'd ever seen. But I needed it to be in the one place I couldn't see it.

We kicked off our boots and sank to the dusty ground. Utterly naked in the jungle, the only noise a distant roar of water and the chirping of birds and insects. David's kiss was all the foreplay I needed and when I spread my legs he was inside me in seconds, his fat, firm cock stretching me inside, filling me up, making me whole. I had never felt so primal, or hungry for another body. I barely knew what I was going to do next, but nature did, as I tilted my hips, letting him spear me as deeply as he possibly could.

We rolled over and over. I lay on top of him, and drew my legs up to my chest before squatting over his cock. I bore down on it with my whole weight, feeling his engorged dick fill me up once more. My clit was so hard and swollen that it jutted out between my pussy lips. David glanced down, saw it, licked his thumb and forefinger and put one on either side of my swollen, yearning clit and rocked his hand gently back and forth, back and forth. His touch was light but the effect was as quick and efficient as flicking an electric light switch. I came hard, barely recognising the animal yowlings I made as my body collapsed on top of his. The spasms came again and again and again. Leaning down towards his face for a final, probing kiss, I abandoned myself to the convulsions.

I dismounted and lay face down next to David, too exhausted to keep fucking. But he hadn't finished with me. His dick was bigger and more turgid than before, bolt upright and thick between his legs. My body was limp, still in recovery from the most powerful orgasm I'd ever known. When he pulled my hips up and slid a knee between my legs to part them I moaned in protest, sure that my fragile, spent body couldn't take any more. But he was inside me before I had a chance to argue, fucking me from behind, thrusting so hard that I couldn't resist and I let myself flop like a rag doll. Agony at having my still-swollen pussy pounded like this soon turned into another sensation, deep inside and towards the front of my body.

It was a shiver that began in my pelvis and flowed along my limbs like a low electric current, numbing my arms and legs, the tingle deep inside me the only sensation I was aware of. The harder David thrust, the more I wanted him to. It was a minute or two before a new rush of pre-orgasmic pleasure indicated that I was about to come again, but this was a different, deeper orgasm than any I'd experienced before. I yielded to the low throb that grew stronger and stronger until I exploded again, feeling a jet of warm liquid emerge from an unknown recess deep inside me. David almost slipped out of me, but my twitching pussy would not release his dick; when he came, he was half-in, half-out of me and I felt two hard jerks before he became absolutely still and cried out in pleasure. My own juices, mixed with his spunk, dribbled out of my cunt and down my thighs, into his pubic hair and made a little puddle on the jungle floor. He tore his dick away from me, and we both rolled on to our backs. We lay side by side, panting, our breathing slowly synchronising just as it had done in the yoga class. That seemed like a lifetime ago now.

The smug arrogance had been replaced by a tenderness that melted me as he kissed me, used his underpants to wipe us both clean and then scampered around the jungle clearing to retrieve our clothing. 'I'm afraid some of these buttons will never come back,' he murmured into my neck as he gently helped me on with my bra before bending down to put my boots back on for me. The kiss he planted on my knee made me shiver with desire again; now that I knew it was possible to come more than once in the same session, I felt that I would always be ready for David.

'So now what?' I said, looking at the sky. 'It'll get dark soon and we've no way of finding our way back.' I was now genuinely worried: we had little water left and, much as I'd like to, we couldn't exist on sex alone.

'Oh, that?' said David, airily, and pushed away a bush to reveal the path that led directly back to our camp. 'I always knew exactly where we were. You were never really lost.'

He couldn't hide his self-satisfied smile for long, and the prickles of irritation began to rise in me again. As I followed him back down to the huts, listening to him brag about the way he'd just made me come twice, I felt more like punching him than kissing him. I gave into it. After all, why try to force myself to like this man when hating him was so much hotter?

THE CAMERA
NEVER LIES

Many of us fantasise about what it would be like to be with another woman. But few of us ever dare to make that fantasy come true. When Sara told me this sizzling Sapphic tale she explained that sometimes events take a completely unexpected turn. All you need to make your own lesbian fantasy come true, she says, is the magic combination of the right place, the right time . . . and, of course, the right woman.

Most girls who are into glamour modelling say they're aspiring catwalk models, or that really they're actresses. Not me. I'm proud of my body and I love to show it off in front of the camera. Modelling is a great way to make a living, and I'm going to milk it for as long as it lasts. I've never been short of work, not since I did my first photoshoot. I'm curvier than your average fashion model, and that works for me. It means I get booked for the straightforward topless shots for men's magazines and also arty shots, videos, quirky adverts where they want a little sex and personality injected into the product.

The images of me might be titillating, but the atmosphere when I'm naked in front of the camera is never uncomfortable or overtly sexy. After all, it's work, I'm a professional and so are the photographers. Besides, most of the guys taking the shots are old enough to be my dad, and they're always protective rather than sleazy.

These days, I pretty much know all the guys who do the glamour stuff, so when I learned that I'd be working with someone I hadn't met before on a job in North London, I was excited. Every new photographer brings out a different side of my personality. But I would never have guessed just what Kim would unleash in me.

The photoshoot was for a new magazine which featured sex articles and erotic stories for women. My job was to model underwear for the fashion spread. I thought it sounded kitsch and glamorous, and when I arrived at the studio, a huge white room in a converted warehouse, I was delighted to see a clothes-rail hung with fabulous, vintage, burlesque-style underwear. The make-up girl and the stylist and I squealed with delight over the classic feminine corsets, the 1940s stockings and sexy fishnets. There was even a beautiful bra and high-waisted panty set made from real parachute silk. I picked the ivory fabric up and held it to my cheek, imagining how light and luxurious it would feel against my body.

We were still rifling through the clothes and discussing which hair and make-up looks to go for when the photographer arrived. A woman who introduced herself as Kim. Not much older than me, she was tall and androgynous with short, light brown hair in an elfin crop. She wore a baggy, masculine pinstripe suit, white Converse sneakers and a tight, white vest. I thought she was one of the coolest-looking people I'd ever seen. Kim was friendly but businesslike and set about creating a mood right away.

'I've brought some music with me,' she said, her tiny features composing themselves into a shy smile. 'It'll transport you back in time – I think it'll really help the atmosphere and we'll get some great pictures.' She popped a CD into the stereo and immediately the gentle strains of a 1940s waltz filled the white-walled room.

Kim busied herself recreating an old-fashioned boudoir with vintage furniture that she arranged in the middle of the studio. Meanwhile, the soft music helped me get into character during the transformation process of hair and make-up. We went for a retro look: pale, powdered skin, lots of kohl eyeliner, mascara and matt red lips. My hair was set on huge rollers and when it was uncurled, the stylist arranged it so that my dark locks tumbled over my shoulders in soft waves. The decades melted away and I looked every inch the burlesque-era startlet.

Kim came up behind me and let her hands rest on my shoulders for a fraction of a second.

'Gorgeous,' she said, brushing a stray strand of hair from my collarbone. 'You look like a forces' sweetheart. Exactly what I was going for.'

She kept her hands on my bare neck while we discussed what she wanted. 'Okay, this is about how sometimes it's the traditional, almost prissy underwear that makes you feel like the most wanton slut of all,' she explained. 'So what we're going to do is start with you in the white stuff, looking quite prim and virginal. And then as we move on to the more racy underwear, we'll muss up your hair and make-up, have you look a bit more wanton and ravaged, so we basically get sexier and more explicit as the story goes on.'

I love to do modelling jobs where I can indulge my theatrical side, so I nodded enthusiastically and told Kim I was looking forward to getting started.

My first costume was a full-length slip with a long, fitted petticoat, a slinky garment which made me yearn for a time when underwear was always subtle and feminine. I thought of the thong and push-up bra I usually wore and resolved to spend my fee from this shoot on something more classically ladylike and luxurious. My picture was taken sitting at an old-fashioned dressing table, combing out my hair with a gorgeous antique silver paddle brush.

'That's great,' said Kim, 'Can you sort of touch the top of your breasts, trail your finger lightly over them? Close your eyes. Think about what it would be like having a lover touch you somewhere intimate.' I hardly needed to imagine it – my fingers were inches away from where Kim had rested her own hand moments before. But in case I needed extra guidance, she used gestures to show me what she wanted. As she slipped out of her jacket, tilted her head back, trailing one hand over a graceful collarbone and let her fingers travel idly down to the gentle curve of her breast, she suddenly looked much softer and more girlish than she'd initially seemed. My subconscious startled me because I immediately wondered what it would be like if I was the one touching her, bringing out that softness in her. I'd never been with a woman before, although I'd fantasised about it. But here in this studio, this fantasy scenario, it felt like anything was possible.

When I posed for the next set of pictures, mimicking that pose with my hand on my breast, it was Kim's hand I imagined touching me. As I let my imagination wander, I felt my nipples harden and poke through the pale pink silk of my slip.

'Is it too cold for you in here?' asked Kim, innocently. I shook my head.

'No, actually, I like that, a nipple hard-on,' she said, training the lens so it focused in on my tits. 'It suggests an inner fantasy life underneath the cutesy, girl-next-door underwear.' Little did she know that *she* was the subject of my fantasies!

When we'd finished that session, Kim downloaded the shots she'd taken so far on to her laptop. We leaned over the computer to look at them. The pictures were gorgeous; a world away from the brash bikini shoots I did for lads' mags. They looked like genuine vintage portraits.

'You have a beautiful body,' said Kim approvingly as she scrolled through image after image of me. 'Not many women these days have that curve there.' She pointed to the sweeping S-shape of my waist on the screen, traced her finger along the lines of my hips, my thighs. I imagined that she was touching me, not my likeness, and the thought of her hands on my arse, my legs, triggered a gentle pulse between my legs.

My next costume was the underwear made from parachute silk. The panties were gossamer light against my skin and the bra was soft, with no underwiring. I liked the way it gently cupped the contours of my body rather than moulding my breasts into two globes. I reclined on a faux-fur rug, stretching my arms all the way up over my head, making sure I struck a different pose with every click of the camera's shutter. Kim kept shouting instructions.

'That's gorgeous, Sara,' she said. 'You're really losing yourself in the fantasy. Now, just hook your thumbs in the top of those panties and pull them down a little bit, show a little bit of skin just above your pussy.'

The word 'pussy' made me blush. Perhaps wearing the delicate underwear from a gentler time was affecting my sensibilities, I told myself with a smile. On her lips, the word was a challenge, a come-on. Was I being ridiculous, letting my fantasy take me over? I didn't even know if Kim was a lesbian or not. Sure, she was kind of boyish, but that didn't mean anything, did it? And even if she was, I wasn't, so why was I thinking about touching her whenever I closed my eyes, yearning to have her climb on this rug and lie next to me?

Kim had me pose on all fours, pouting at the camera, arse sticking up in the air. The strong photographer's lights shone on my legs and thighs, creating the same pleasant fuzzy, horny sensation you get from lying in the sun.

'Oh, beautiful, beautiful,' said Kim. The more she complimented me, the more sensual I felt. I slithered around on that rug, then knelt with my legs apart, raising my arms above my head.

'Beautiful,' said Kim again and then, 'I'm going to set the camera to automatic so it just fires off loads of shots, so we should get you doing some spontaneous movements. Just do more of what you were doing, show off that stunning figure of yours.' Kim crouched next to the camera while it clicked away.

She really was very beautiful, with feline features that let her carry off that boyish crop. And her body was sexy too: her arms were slim, but sinewy and muscular. Next to those worked-out arms, the soft swell of her breasts was even more arousing. She wore no bra under her vest top. I wanted to make those nipples hard. I wanted to make her pussy wet.

I decided to tease her a little, see if I could affect her the way she'd affected me. I sunk down on my thighs, spreading myself even wider and sticking out my tits, so the milky white skin between my legs was exposed. I closed my eyes, put a finger between my lips and bit down on it.

When I looked back at Kim, her tits were definitely getting hard, her lips looked bigger and redder, and her eyes were shining. I wondered what she was feeling. What was happening between her legs? Was it anything like the urgent, pulsing beat that throbbed between mine?

After we'd finished that set of pictures, I returned to the changing room and slipped off my silken ivory knickers. I pressed them to my nose and breathed in my own scent, the fresh, musky aroma a clear sign of my arousal. Suddenly I wanted to smell that same smell on Kim, to put my face in her panties and between her legs. I'd never felt the urge to do that with another woman before: now it was *all* I wanted to do.

My final costume was a much sexier bustier-and-suspender set, baby-blue, with a billowing pair of French knickers. There was nothing innocent about this ensemble. My outfit was topped off by American Tan stockings complete with a black seam up the back, and pale blue, round-toed shoes and chunky heels. I looked like Betty Grable. When I sauntered back across the studio, Kim let out a low whistle.

'Oh wow! This is it! *This* is the cover shot,' she said, excitedly, dimming the lights. I reclined on the old-fashioned brass bed, enjoying the cool satin of the divan against my skin. I squeezed my thighs together so that the folds of the knickers bunched up and caressed my clitoris.

'Okay, we're ready,' said Kim, and I was off. I posed and preened, swaying in time to the music and coming alive under Kim's murmurs of encouragement. As the record ended, Kim too fell silent, lost in the performance I was putting on just for her. The silent studio echoed with no other sounds than the click of the camera, the swish of satin on skin and the noise of two women breathing hard.

'Let's try a couple without the shoes and stockings now,' suggested Kim.

I'd done some burlesque stripping before and knew exactly how to undress a leg in the most sexy and tantalising way. I elegantly stuck my foot out in front of me, then kicked my shoe across the room, letting the remaining shoe dangle off my toe so that it flattered my slender ankles before letting it fall to the floor. Next I stood up and, looking right at the lens, removed first one, then another suspender clip, touching myself as I did so. I bent down so that Kim could see down my bra and then slowly, so tantalisingly slowly that it tickled every inch of the way, I rolled one stocking down my leg before elegantly pulling it off and hanging it over the edge of the bed, where it still retained the shape of my leg. Then I turned my back to the camera so it – and Kim – could see my arse as I bent down and rolled the other stocking, making sure my hands smoothed over my legs and caressed them as I moved along. I parted my legs and made a peekaboo face through my thighs at the camera, winking at the lens.

'Great shot,' said Kim, and her voice came out in a low rasp that made me shiver from head to toe. I lay down on the bed, pointed my feet in the air, rolled over so I was face down and rubbed myself against the pillow, feeling its soft bulk against my swollen, excited clit. I sat up facing the camera and ran my fingers over my nipples, licked one finger and then slid it under my bra, flicking my nipple and sighing with pleasure. Behind the camera, I saw Kim's hand instinctively go to her own breast. Her strong, muscular hand on that soft breast was such a turn-on that I had to bite down on my lip to stop myself from crying out, begging her to come and touch me. If I couldn't bring myself to say it with words, I would issue an invitation with my body that she couldn't refuse.

Encouraged by the expression on Kim's face and her short, shallow breathing, I removed my bra, my tits round, firm and warm under the studio lights. When she saw my breasts for the first time, Kim let out a whimper. I hung the bra over the edge of the bed with the stockings. Then, lying on my back, I put my feet in the air and pulled the French knickers over my legs so that I was naked but for the pale blue, lacy suspender belt. The camera was still clicking, but at less frequent intervals now; Kim was so captivated by the scene in front of her that she struggled to concentrate on the photography.

Emboldened by sheer desire – mine and hers – I climbed down from the bed and slowly undid my suspender belt, letting it fall to the floor. As if in a trance, I walked over to the middle of the studio and beckoned Kim over. As she approached me, she looked so deliciously young and vulnerable. As soon as she was near enough to touch, I wrapped my arms around her waist and pulled her towards me. She was trembling as I gently pressed my lips to hers.

Kim was almost exactly my height and not far off my weight; I was used to feeling dwarfed by men who were bigger, hairier, rougher than me. Standing face to face with another woman, my physical equal, was an incredibly erotic sensation. She soon relaxed in my arms and kissed me back with a depth and passion that was more than a match for mine. I slid my hands under her vest and she lifted her arms above her head so that I could pull the garment off her in one swift movement. I took a few seconds to enjoy the sight of her breasts, soft, round and high, a delicious feminine swelling on a lithe, toned body.

We kissed again, the hard buds of her nipples rubbing deliciously against mine, our tits pressing together as our bodies moved in closer and tighter. I helped Kim to wriggle out of her clothes, tugging at her trousers, frantically pulling at her panties until we were both naked, my waxed, smooth pussy enjoying the friction as I rubbed it against her neatly trimmed bush, our juices mingling together. Her hands trailed lightly up and down my spine, making me shiver with desire.

Kim took charge now, leading me by the hand to the bed. We collapsed on to the rumpled bedclothes, a tangle of sheets, tits, arms and legs, every inch of my skin on fire. She lay on top of me, the light weight of her body pinning me down. Hoping that she would follow my lead, I slid my hand between her legs which she spread eagerly. For the first time in my life I was touching another woman's pussy and it felt soft, wet, warm and welcoming. With my thumb gently flicking Kim's clitoris, I used my fingers to trace the outline of her pussy lips before sliding a couple of fingers inside her tight, wet hole. She whimpered with pleasure, biting down on my shoulder and shuddering as her sex quivered around my fingers. I pulled my hand away, using her natural juices to moisten her clitoris so that I could rub it harder, faster. To my delight, the little bud grew even more swollen under my touch. The harder I rubbed her clit, the more I wanted her to touch mine.

As if reading my mind, Kim pulled away and lay on her back, her pussy making a delicate kissing noise as she slithered away from my fingers. I put my hand to my nose and breathed in her scent, far more arousing and enticing than any manufactured perfume could ever be. I closed my eyes and inhaled deeply. When I opened them, Kim lay at my knees, strong wiry arms forcing my thighs apart. I felt my cunt pound in anticipation, so fast and hard that I was sure she could see it.

Kim licked every inch of my thighs, my slit, my pudenda: I'd had the whole area waxed a couple of days ago so the hairless mound was as sensitive to the touch as it could possibly be. I felt her lips, her tongue, the odd teasing tickle of teeth as she devoured me.

I spread my legs, my proud, throbbing little clit protruding, begging for her attention. Kim went to work, making a little pointed rosebud of her tongue which darted all over my clit. Never breaking contact between my pussy and her mouth, she turned her entire body around, swinging her leg over my shoulder so that her knees were either side of my chest and her arse hovered a few inches over my breasts. Eagerly I licked my fingers and eased my hand through her parted thighs. I had easy access to her whole vulva and I rubbed enthusiastically at her flesh, flicking her clit and fingering her slit. She bucked and writhed with pleasure as we both stepped up the pace, me jabbing at her with an excited hand, her tongue flickering all over my blissed-out pussy.

My body became a white ball of heat just waiting to explode as Kim's tongue teased and pleased me. She came first: her body suddenly became motionless, then there was a brief spasm, and a warm trickle of her juices ran down the inside of my wrist. As she climaxed, she sucked hard on the tip of my clitoris, producing the most intense, exquisite tension I have ever known. When I let go and surrendered to my orgasm, my body went into meltdown.

Both spent by our climaxes, we drifted off to sleep on the bed. When I awoke, Kim was nuzzling at my breast with her perfect gamine pout.

'Ready for round two?' she said mischievously. I nodded, ready for the flick of her tongue, eager this time to taste as well as smell her.

'There's just one thing,' she said. 'The camera loves you. So it would be a terrible shame to waste this opportunity.'

She leapt up, dashed across to the camera, and set it to auto. The random shutter clicks began and we reached for each other. I parted Kim's legs, stared at that beautiful pink pussy and got ready to give the performance of a lifetime.

FETISH

I met Polly, a beautiful British student, when she was wait-
ressing in a restaurant in Oxford. Over coffee, she told me of
an erotic encounter she'd had whilst working abroad, in a very
different kind of establishment. I found her story so arousing
and inspiring that I rushed out and bought myself a whole
wardrobe of fetish clothing the very next day. The kinky pleas-
ures of a little leather and rubber against the skin will awaken
dark desires in everyone. It worked for Polly, and it worked
for me. Why not find out if it works for you, too?

I sprinkle the talcum powder on to my breasts, sides and
underarms so that my skin-tight latex top slides on easily.
I pull it over my breasts, enjoying the sensation as my
nipples disappear into the tight, suffocating, stretchy material. I love to dress for work in front of the mirror. Tonight,
I'm wearing black. I study my reflection, legs apart, naked
but for a black top that clings like a second skin, no,
tighter than that, because tiny bulges of flesh spill over
the top of the boob tube.

The first time I wore a dress made out of rubber was my first night working in the bar. I pulled it straight on, no baby powder, no oil to stop the material scraping my skin. It took a week for the red marks to fade. Not that it mattered much. The clients here like that sort of thing. My coal-dark, raven hair is sliced into a Louise Brooks bob. My tidy little bush, trimmed with a razor this morning, is also jet-black. I look hot. It's almost a shame I have to put my skirt on, but even a club as liberal as mine doesn't let you serve drinks naked from the waist down.

I smile to myself at this as I zip the black leather hotpants up. They fasten at the sides, so they follow perfectly the curve of my hips. I don't wear panties beneath them; the shorts are so brief and tight that there isn't room for underwear. They would bunch and ruin the perfect smooth line. I like the way the leather sculpts my buttocks into a perfect, uninterrupted arc. And there's another reason why knickers aren't an option under these hotpants. These shorts are lined with leather, and when I get wet – which happens a lot, I'm a very sexual person – the leather doesn't absorb my juices, but lets them slide around, making me hotter and wetter.

I check my pedicure before pulling on my boots: lily-white feet jewelled with scarlet-painted toes, the same shade as my fingernails, which I keep short and neat. No one else will see my feet, but I like to know my look is perfect from head to toe. Only when I'm satisfied do the boots go on. Oh, these boots! I want to be buried in them. Black PVC, thigh-high with a silver stiletto that makes me walk with a wiggle, tits and arse sticking out for all to admire. As I zip them up, the cold plastic feels like a lover's caress on my calves.

Nearly ready to play. It's just time for my finishing touch, my signature style. My own customised rubber gauntlets. They're like long evening gloves, but they don't cover my hands. Instead they bind me from wrist to upper arm. I made them myself from a length of rubber I bought in my favourite fetish shop. When I'm wearing them, I can't quite bend my arms properly. I love that tiny restriction: it means I always concentrate on my job, I never get to be totally at ease with my body. I feel my flesh begin to heat up. In a few minutes, the sweat underneath will have broken through the talcum powder and that delicious discomfort will begin, and it won't end until I get out of my costume and into the shower at the end of my shift.

Final glance in the mirror and I apply the red lipstick that says, 'fuck with me, but don't kiss me'. I look angular, geometric. Sometimes I feel that the real pleasure is in putting the clothes on. Sure, I often meet guys who I like the look of when I'm working, and God knows I get plenty of offers, but I love my job and I'd never do anything to jeopardise it. Work is work. I can find sex in my free time.

When my mother advised me to get a bar job to tide me over on my year studying German at Hamburg University, I'm not sure this was what she had in mind. She doesn't know that I work at Bar Fetisch on the notorious Reeperbhan, right in the middle of the red-light district. But hey, I live above the club, I'm learning the language and I pour a great glass of beer. And because I'm 100 per cent wipe-clean, it doesn't matter if I drop it.

A glance at the clock tells me my shift begins in sixty seconds. I totter down the stairs on my vertiginous heels, through the door marked 'Staff Only', down a dim, red corridor and then through the beaded curtain and *It's Showtime*! It's 10 p.m. but the night has barely started yet. Claudia, my manager, is doing the same shift as me and is already behind the bar. When we check out each other's 'uniform', we burst into spontaneous laughter. She's dressed like a mirror image of me but the colours are reversed; she wears all-over crimson: boob tube, hotpants and boots, and she's got this fabulous, blood-red bobbed wig I've never seen her wear before. I love it. She even has on black lipstick and inky-dark nail varnish. Her generous tits are almost flattened by the latex that binds her chest and threatens to suffocate her skin.

'You look sensational!' I tell her.

'*Danke*,' she replies. (Claudia has made it her project to finesse my German skills before term starts.) 'We'll have to make sure we stick together tonight. Once the customers see the way we look next to each other, we'll be stuffing tips into our clothes.'

'Oh *dear*,' I say, making a pretend sad face. 'I don't think I can fit anything else between my skin and these clothes.'

'Where there's a will, there's a way!' says Claudia, before turning her dazzling smile on a guy who's just walked in.

When I first met Claudia, her confidence and sass just blew me away. For a while I even had a kind of crush on her, but it never became physical, and now I'm glad about that. I'm up for anything, but when it comes to sex, I'm all about the dick.

I take a tray and walk around the bar, collecting empty glasses and wiping down the surfaces. You'd be astonished at the kind of things I've had to clean off the furniture in this job. It's not unheard of to see couples fucking on the side of the stage where they think we can't see them, or for frantic hands to make desperate grabs under tables. Of course, I can't see what's happening under the tables, but faces give more away than bodies do; I can spot someone having an orgasm from twenty paces now – just by the look on their faces. I used to get turned on by it at first, but I'm kind of blasé now.

On a rammed night like this, the hours fly by. There's the usual mix of customers, mostly a fetish crowd, who I know and say hello to. There's a guy called Antoine, who's actually French but loves the bondage scene so much he moved here. Not my type, though: he's very smooth-bodied and slender and I like my men rough, hairy, unclean. I spend some time at the bar, passing time with Helena and Guy, a couple in their mid-thirties who steal away to the bar whenever they can get a babysitter and relive the fetish clubbing days of their early courtship. Helena can still fit into her original 1980s dress. Guy describes how it takes an hour to buckle and belt her into it, not because fastening the various catches is labor-ious, but because the sight of her trussed up in rubber is so horny he'll stop to fuck her twice, once in the pussy and once in the face. He doesn't hold back on any of the details, and my nipples get hard and hot under my rubber bandeau.

The usual collection of tourists dressed in street clothes are in tonight. They fall into two categories: the ones who look around them, immediately either blush or mumble an excuse, and then turn on their heels and run out. Then there are those whose eyes widen, who edge shyly forward, taking in the mix of people and letting the banging industrial music take over as they nervously order a beer. I always make a special point of talking to these customers to put them at their ease, and not just because I want their tips: you don't do this job unless you're curious about people and what makes them tick. My favourite kind of customer, the one who turns up in jeans and a T-shirt, is the one who, come 4 a.m., is doing tequila shots and frantically snogging some fetish-head in full-body latex. There's nothing like your first night in the world of kink.

At midnight, the place really gets going: every table is packed out, a sea of flesh wrapped in black and red gear. Tray balancing on my shoulder, I squeeze my way through the crowd, the bare flesh on my thighs and belly occasionally brushes against someone's fetish wear, waking up my skin, making me feel alive. We turn the music up so loud that we have to lip-read each other, and if you stand too near the speakers the bass is so strong you feel it in your pussy. A crowd starts to sway on the tiny dance floor, men and women working up a sweat that gathers in pools under their restrictive clothes. The place smells hot, sexy, of skin and rubber. I look around the packed room, checking there are no glasses or ashtrays that need emptying. Not many tourists in tonight, just the usual fetish crowd, old friends greeting each other, new friends being made, flirting and little sexual intrigues developing all over the place. On nights like this, I have the best job in the world. I scan the room again, this time observing people's faces. Relaxation, excitement, trepidation, adventure; everyone's features tell a different, fascinating story.

Then I do a double take. There's one face in the crowd that isn't joining in, isn't watching anyone. A man, early twenties, a pale, almost aristocratic, English-looking face with steely blue eyes that don't smile. Thick, light-brown wavy hair brushes the collarbone of his black polo neck sweater. He's also wearing black needlecord trousers and smart boots. I can tell that his clothes are made of cashmere, fine cotton and softest nubuck leather. I don't know what to make of him; he looks more like an escaped librarian than a clubber or a regular on the fetish scene. He looks cultured. Rich. Uptight, even. What the hell's he doing here? I decide to break the ice.

'Hi,' I say to him in German, sidling over to his table. 'How are you? What are you drinking? Can I get you another?' I ask, even though his beer is still virtually untouched. 'Is this your first time here?' The closer I get to him, the more I talk, always a sign that I'm feeling nervous about something. Something about this fusty young man is compelling. I like the way he smells. I like his face. For the first time in years, I'm reminded of the random nature and irresistible pull of sexual chemistry. I'm disarmed by a sudden rush of lust and adrenaline that makes me sway, shudder and nearly drop my tray. When he opens his soft lips to speak, a familiar fluttering in my pussy takes me by surprise.

'I'm Florian,' he says, ignoring all my questions. 'And you are very beautiful.' He places a hand on my naked stomach. Usually behaviour like this from a customer I don't know (or even one that I do) would not be tolerated, he would get a slap in the face and Claudia and I would throw him out on the pavement. I'm a waitress, not a private dancer, after all.

But for some reason I don't shrink from his touch. Because when his hand makes contact with my skin, it's as intense and surprising as being branded with a white-hot poker. His fingertips on my stomach send a searing shock of electricity through my whole body, little lightning rods of sexual desire. He watches as my nipples make hard little buds under my top. I gasp for breath as a hot, sticky, trickle of liquid slithers out of my pussy and pools in the gusset of my leather shorts. This is all happening so fast: usually it takes a couple of dates, some fooling around, a little kissing to get me this horny.

Florian hooks one finger under the bottom of my boob tube and stretches the rubber out a little, letting a cool vent of air shoot up between my aching tits. Then he lets the material go so that my top snaps back on to my body, a stinging sensation that I like. That I like a little too much: I'm completely out of my depth here.

Feeling the need to calm down, I walk away from this odd guy and back through the crowd, taking drinks orders and chatting to the regulars.

I work harder than ever that night, making sure the bar is fully stocked, wiping it down, collecting glasses but letting Claudia look after Florian. I watch as she refreshes his glass a couple of times; he doesn't touch or stare at her, but treats her with respect and detachment. His eyes are boring into me, burning holes in my flesh as real and intense as the pain he caused when he pinged my top. With shaky hands, I reapply my red lipstick in the mirror behind the bar; through the dark sea of faces I register his pale eyes watching me. I'm scared at how much I'm feeling for a guy I don't know. I'm frightened of what happens if I act on this unprecedented impulse to pull his fine clothes slowly off his strong but soft body while he rips off my fetish gear. It's like I've swallowed some unfamiliar drug, and I don't know what the side effects will be. I avoid him, hoping it will go away on its own.

I'm about to check the ladies' bathroom for discarded glasses when he walks out of the men's room.

'I've never seen skin that white against such black leather,' he says, not touching me this time, although I want him to so much it's all I can do not to grab his hand and place it against my skin. 'I can see the shape of your nipples,' he continues. 'They're big, and getting bigger as

I talk to you. But I wonder what colour they are. Will they be pale, like your thighs? Dark, like your hair and your eyes? Or red, like your lips?'

Without waiting for a reply, he turns on his heel and leaves me gasping and panting and throbbing so hard between my legs that I'm sure my swollen pussy must be bulging in my skimpy hotpants, my arousal plain to see. My concentration is shot for the rest of the night. When I work the till, the numbers swim before my eyes.

'Are you okay?' asks Claudia, when I start to mess up on drinks orders.

'Fine,' I say. 'A little hot, that's all.'

'Take a break,' she says. 'I can handle it in here. You've worked so hard, the place is spotless and everyone's got drinks lined up for at least half an hour. Go and get some fresh air.'

I try to protest, but she slaps my thigh and shoos me out the back. 'It's an order!' she shouts. 'I need a waitress who's on top of things. Go!'

I slip through the staff door and then through the beaded curtain into the relative cool and fresh air of the wooden staircase that links the main club to my little studio apartment. I sit down on the step with a thud, grateful for the breeze on my skin. I hear the thud-thud-thud of our banging techno music through the wall, and my throbbing pussy seems to keep time to it. I rock back and forth, my clitoris and pussy lips squeezed so tight, bound so closely by my second-skin leather hotpants that I think if I just press my thighs together enough and rock back and forth for just half a minute, I'll give myself the orgasm I need and I can get back to work. No one's watching. I decide to go for it. I shut my eyes, begin to tilt my body back and forth, back and forth, feeling the climax begin to well up between my legs as shivers run the length of my limbs.

I'm seconds from getting myself off when the swish of the curtain makes me open my eyes. How the fuck did he get back here? He must have watched and followed me.

'So,' he says, as though I've been expecting him, and in a way I have. 'So.' And he advances forward, so that his hips are level with my eyes.

He extends one long, elegant finger and runs it over my breasts. It squeaks on the damp latex. My skin beneath my clothes turns to ice, then fire. He finds my nipple and pushes it in hard, his finger making a little depression in the round dome of flesh, then releasing it just as it begins to hurt.

He holds my wrists, encased in more black latex and pulls them over my head. And all the while I let him. I think I will let him do whatever he wants to me. Without warning, he pulls me to my feet. I'm tall in my spiked boots, we're eye-to-eye for a few seconds and then he bares his teeth and swoops on my breasts like a vampire, biting my tits through the latex, making me cry out with pleasure so loudly I'm sure they can hear me in the club.

He traces his tongue along my top and licks, kisses and sucks all the way up my collarbone, stopping to inhale deeply in my armpit. He slides his tongue underneath the rim of my armband, hands on my waist now, kneading my bare flesh while his mouth devours me.

'I want to see your tits,' he says, and pulls off my top, yanking it violently down and away from my skin. My flesh stings as the rubber is peeled off in one swift, merciless movement. The bandeau makes a roll around my middle, squeezing out the flesh above and below it. I look down at my exposed tits. Without the support of the top, they're an inch or two lower than when bound in the latex and about three sizes bigger. My white skin is scarred with red bite marks and latex burns and my nipples, usually palest pink, are engorged and have become the shade of a dark damask rose. They swell and harden, craving more of Florian's lips. He gratifies them, bending down to bite, suckle and inhale. As his tongue traces whorls around my areola, I know that he's enjoying the bitter aftertaste of the latex was well as the natural oils of my flesh.

'You taste and smell as beautiful as you look,' he snarls. 'And soon I'm going to know what it feels like to fuck you. But first, I need to see some more skin.' His eyes dart around the small corridor, stacked with crates, before alighting on a small craft knife that we use to slice open boxes. His face breaks into a cruel little smile. I'm turned on, but panicking, too. I'm so horny I'll let him do whatever he wants . . . but *cut* me? But it's not me he wants to cut. Florian runs the blade down first one armband, then the other, slicing the tight cuffs open. The cold steel of the blade teases my skin as the rubber springs back, exposing the damp, pale flesh of my inner arms to the cold night air.

He pushes me down against the stairs again, my now naked back in contact with the cold, unforgiving wooden steps. My flesh, already sore from the skiddy latex, jags against the harsh surface. Florian kneels between my knees, puts his head between my legs and snuffles like a puppy.

Even I can smell how turned on I am, and he can too; it's driving him mad, he bites at the crotch of my shorts trying to pull the gusset aside and fuck me with his tongue, but they're too tight, he can't do it.

My clit's throbbing so much I think I'll pass out if I don't feel him on me, in me, soon, now. His hands tear at the leather, fingers digging painfully into the tender flesh of my inner thigh as he grapples with the unyielding hide to no avail. I grab his hands and place them on the twin zips that fasten the shorts so tightly to my body.

Hooking his forefingers into the loops, he pulls the zips down, peels back the fabric and exposes my damp, soaked bush and a very red and swollen pussy.

He touches my clit with the tip of his nose. His warm breath on my flesh combined with the smell of my own pussy rising into the air is the purest aphrodisiac I've ever known. Still prodding my clit with his nose, he licks up what juices he can from my twitching pussy. I'm so turned on and so wet that whatever he drinks up, I produce more. I'm dangerously close to coming as he hardens his tongue and probes the first couple of inches of my slit. I want to come; but I want him inside me, too.

This is when he takes his head away and opens his fly to reveal a quivering, smooth cock that bobs inches from my eyes. I gaze at the beautiful silken skin and the lone vein that throbs and pounds along the length of it.

'I don't know whether to fuck you in that beautiful red mouth or in that beautiful red cunt,' he says idly. I open my mouth to beg him to fuck me in the pussy, but he sticks his cock between my lips and thrusts hard against the back of my throat, his dick silencing me. I am helpless before him, naked except for my boots, as he deepthroats me. I let my body turn to jelly; he can do whatever he likes. When I think I'm about to pass out, he pulls his dick out of me. A red lipstick ring decorates the base of his cock and the top of his balls. He pulls me by the hair so that I'm on my feet again; without letting go of my hair, he jabs his hard-on between my legs. Our bodies fit together perfectly, smoothly, and when he fills me up, I whimper with pleasure. I lean against him, our bodies pressed together, my tits on his chest, my clit grinding into him. I've held off my orgasm for long enough, I think, as he spears into me again and again and again. Then I come, once, twice, three times: a tsunami of pleasure washes over my body. I want to feel his own juices spurt and warm up my insides but he pulls out and shoots his spunk into my chest.

Florian's dick is still oozing pearly liquid when he wrestles my boob tube back up over my body, stretching it over my tits so that his semen is trapped between my skin and the thin layer of latex. As I retrieve my shorts from around my knees, he kisses my stomach slowly, his gentle touch gradually bringing me back down to earth and soothing the scorch marks of his earlier touches. Finally he wipes the smeared lipstick from my face. Without a backward glance, he swishes through the curtain and goes back into the club, leaving me in a tingling heap on the stairs, his cum cooling on my tits and inside my shorts.

When I come back into the club, Claudia looks up sharply. 'Why are you back so quickly?' she admonishes me. 'I said take a good fifteen minutes!' And then, looking me up and down again, 'What happened to your armbands?'

I look at the clock in disbelief. I've been gone less than five minutes. Only the sticky spunk against my skin and the taste of his cock on my lips tells me I didn't imagine the whole thing. I scan the dark club. Happy, smiling people throng the room. He isn't one of them. But he'll be back. I know it.

THE CAPTAIN'S TABLE

Who hasn't dreamed of finding a world where anything goes, where you can voice your most extreme sexual desires without being judged, where a constant supply of new, willing lovers is always on hand? It sounds too good to be true, but these places do exist. You just have to know where to look for them.

Charmaine had always dreamed of finding people like herself, people who wanted to swap sensual experiences, who would let her indulge her curiosity for other men and women. When her lover found a cruise ship that was strictly adults only she found her own idea of heaven here on earth. Well, on the sea . . .

'A cruise?' I looked at Ben in disbelief. He was supposed to be my sex slave, my partner in crime, my beautiful boy. And for our first holiday in years, he'd booked us on a cruise, which would be full of old women playing bingo and fat, ancient men sunbathing in string vests. 'You've booked us on a cruise? What next? Pipe and slippers?' I stormed off upstairs to the bedroom, regretting the decision to hand our vacation planning over to him. I'd wanted somewhere exotic, earthy, sexy; a bit of sensual luxury in the Maldives, maybe, or a vibrant city packed with sex clubs like Paris. But a bloody *cruise*?

Ben took my outburst in good humour. 'Trust me, Charmaine,' he said. 'I promise it'll be fun. Have I ever let you down before?'

He hadn't, of course. Usually Ben's surprises were highly sexy and creative, but something as mundane as a cruise was totally out of character.

Ben followed me upstairs and slid a brochure in my direction.

'Trust me,' he said. 'Just look at where I'm taking you. And then tell me if you still think I'm ready for a pipe and slippers.'

He pushed the glossy, slim brochure across the duvet to me. Instead of being decorated with pictures of middle-aged men and women, the cover depicted a gang of glorious bodies, all entwined on the same sun-lounger, looking bronzed and relaxed. And then I saw what it said.

'The Swinging Ship,' it read. 'The cruise company where *anything* goes.'

Intrigued, I flipped through the pages and discovered that this wasn't just any old cruise around the Mediterranean. This was a sex cruise, a couples-only floating paradise for those who want to experiment with their bodies – and other people's, too. Idle browsing turned to serious interest as I read about nightclub rooms where clothing was optional, a huge sauna complex and luxurious cabins with beds large enough for six or seven people. Glossy pictures of young, attractive couples from all over Europe illustrated the brochure. I'd always loved the idea of going to an orgy, and now Ben had decided to make my fantasy a reality. I pictured myself and Ben among their number and looked up to see him standing in the doorway, a sure smile on his face.

'You clever bastard,' I said. 'Now come here and let me say thank you.' I hitched up my skirt and we fucked on our bed there and then. Ben lay on top, his chunky body crushing the breath out of me as he whispered in my ear about how horny it would be when we saw other couples fucking. He told me how he couldn't wait to show me off to all those other men. The more he talked, the more I lost myself in the fantasy; when I came, about thirty seconds after he penetrated me, it was the strongest, sweetest orgasm I'd had for years.

Before we left, I visited my favourite lingerie boutique and picked up several exquisite designer bikinis, scraps of lycra in vibrant colours, barely held together with wisps of string and lace. They left nothing about my body to the imagination. If I was going to spend the next week wearing very little, then I wanted what little I did wear to be sensational. I read and reread the brochure, so excited that I didn't know what aspect of the ship I would enjoy exploring the most. I decided that I was going to try everything, from the sex swing in the ship's dungeon, to the naked sauna, to the nude sunbathing. Oh, Ben and I were going to have the holiday of our lives together! For the next day or so I was constantly wet just at the thought of it. I could have made love to Ben ten times a day but I decided to abstain before the holiday, to let the exquisite tension build up. We didn't discuss it, but I knew Ben felt the same; after five years we knew each other inside out.

We flew to the south of France and boarded the ship in a private harbour near Nice. I'd never been up close to a cruise liner before and it was vast, like a floating hotel. Lights twinkled from windows and it was thrilling to think of all the adventures that lay in store for us on deck. Walking up the gangplank we noticed an extremely glamorous couple who had been on our flight. Both were tall and slender: he had olive skin and piercing blue eyes under jet-black eyebrows while she was as pale as he was tanned with long red hair that wound down her back in flaming ropes.

'Well,' Ben said, watching me devour their bodies with my eyes, 'If all the clientele are this sexy, I think we're going to have a rather wonderful time.'

Our cabin was, as promised, beautiful, with dark, dramatic, gothic decor; deep-red walls, arched mirrors and black, wrought-iron candelabras hanging from the ceiling. The cabin was dominated by a vast iron bed. It was thrilling to be here but as Ben and I dressed for dinner, we were suddenly nervous, too. This was something we'd always talked about, but now we were here we felt like two kids on their first day of school. What if the other couples didn't want to play with us? What if we didn't want to play with them? We were after a fun, sexy, anything-goes atmosphere – but what if other people's idea of 'swinging' was dark and sinister? Our arousal was masked by a shared sense of trepidation.

Once we left the cabin, we began to feel immediately better. In the gangways and on deck, everyone smiled and said hello. The sun was setting as cocktail hour began and it was clear that everyone was dressed to impress. Women and men alike wore dramatic, revealing clothes and there was a flirty, fun atmosphere in the air.

Dinner was a formal affair, held in the ship's banqueting hall. We sipped cocktails while studying the seating plan, looking for our names. We finally took our places opposite Willem and Nina, a friendly couple from Holland. Like us, they were in their late twenties, but it was their third time on the cruise. 'We'll never go on holiday anywhere else,' they said, but before they could divulge anything more the sound of a fork tapping a wine glass called us to attention and made us all turn towards the stage at one end of the hall. A devastatingly handsome man with cropped, light brown hair was standing on a podium. He was dressed in a traditional white captain's uniform complete with peaked cap. Beside him stood a beautiful Asian woman, her expensively highlighted hair the same colour as her smooth and creamy skin.

'Ladies and gentlemen,' said the uniformed man into a microphone. 'Hello, and welcome to the best week of your lives. I'm Adam, and I'm the Captain of your ship. This is my wife Suki,' at this, Suki raised a slender arm in a graceful wave. 'We've got a lot of fun things laid on for you this week, and we want you to feel that you can ask us anything. It's up to you – you can do as little as you wish or as much as you can handle.' A ripple of laughter echoed around the room. 'I just want to announce a few ship rules. First of all, this is a cruise for consenting adults. We're all here to have a good time, so no one is able to judge anything that other consenting adults do for pleasure. We're here to get away from the narrow-minded attitudes of the general public who don't understand – poor things – just how far you can take sex-play and all the wonderful sensations you can experience.' There was a small round of applause and a couple of people cheered. 'But that goes both ways,' continued Adam. 'At no point is it acceptable for any of our guests to pressure another passenger into participating in something which makes them feel uncomfortable. On the ship we have a code: if you're not comfortable with something or someone, you simply remove their hand and say, no, that's not for me. Failure to respect another guest's privacy like this will result in you being ejected from the cruise.'

Ben slid his arm around my waist. I could tell that he was forgetting his nervousness and growing curious and excited, like me. Even hearing Adam describe the ship's activities was a turn on. I felt my nipples begin to harden and I grabbed Ben's hand and held it between my legs so that he could feel the low throb of my awakening clitoris.

Now it was Suki's turn to step up to the mic.

'That's really all we have to say,' she said. 'Although we're here to help with any questions you have. And the final thing is to remember that this is an all-inclusive holiday. That means you don't have to pay for any food, drink, condoms or lube on board. Feel free to consume as much as you like of any of them. And have a wonderful, delicious holiday full of new sensations!'

This time the round of applause was louder and Ben and I joined in. Over a steak dinner we got chatting more to Willem and Nina. It was fascinating to hear their words of experience.

'Adam and Suki control the Captain's Table,' explained

Nina. 'Every evening, they invite one or two couples they like the look of to dine with them. And then the partying goes on in their suite way into the night.'

Ben and I looked again at the Captain and his wife, both so confident and sexy. I knew that, like me, he was wondering what it would be like to fuck them, to swap partners, to watch them fuck and have them watch us. I knew what he was thinking because my hand was resting on his lap and I could feel his dick growing rock hard as Willem carried on explaining.

'Last time we were here, we dined with them one night. It was the most intense night of my whole life. I'll never forget it.' And with the memory of it obviously overwhelming them, he and Nina leaned in and gave each other a lingering, intimate kiss. He slid his hand under her top, lifted her breast to his lips and began to suck her nipple. I shivered with shock and excitement. Sure I've watched porn and seen other people have sex. I've sat behind teenagers dry-humping on the night bus, but I'd never been so close to two other people like that before – freely indulging in foreplay before my eyes. My own nipples began to harden and I felt Ben's cock strain and bounce, ready for action. I gave the sensitive tip of his penis a squeeze. We ate the rest of dinner with Nina's round, bulbous breast exposed. Ben couldn't take his eyes of it and neither could I. I'd never been that near another woman's naked breast before and it was wildly distracting. As I sipped my wine, I wondered idly what it would be like to put that breast in my mouth and gently suck on it, teasing it with my tongue, seeing how big and hard I could make that nipple go.

After dinner we wandered around the ship. The stars twinkled in the sky above us and cast tiny dancing reflections on the inky surface of the Mediterranean. Fairylights gave a soft, sensual glow to everything on deck. The atmosphere was now more overtly sexy. A pretty, petite French woman placed her hand on Ben's thigh as we stood in front of a large display detailing all the different nights and activities available on board. It sent a sizzle of excitement up and down my spine and between my legs. It didn't mean anything was going to happen between us; it just meant it was an attractive woman wanting to touch an attractive man. All the usual rules didn't apply here.

There were so many activities to choose from, I didn't know where to start. In the end, we decided to chill out in the ship's sauna. We'd heard it was a great meeting place and also it would relax us. We wandered down to the fitness suite, exchanged our clothes, which we placed in a locker, for a pristine white towel that did little to cover one's modesty – but that was the idea. After trying and failing to fasten the towels around our bodies, Ben and I shrugged and threw them over our shoulders, trying to look cool and nonchalant as we strode through the sauna. It was the first time we'd been naked together in public, and I loved it immediately: the warm, steamy air on my skin, the sense of freedom, the heat radiating from Ben's body next to mine. And I loved the admiring glances we were getting from strangers, both male and female.

Ben opened a glass door into the steam room; misty heat made my muscles relax and sweat ran down our bodies. The sauna itself was as pristine as any upscale health spa, with gleaming white tiles, polished marble and smooth, blond wood. Couples lolled about in whatever position felt comfortable. We reclined on our towels, watching others come and go. A black couple kissed passionately on a bench a few yards away, and when another man and a woman came up and started touching the black woman's tits, she moaned softly with pleasure. Slowly all four of them became entwined, dark brown and pale pink flesh making a Celtic knot of human bodies. As we watched them, Ben and I instinctively grabbed each other's genitals. I massaged his dick into a rock-hard pole, and he fondled my clit until I had to bite my lip and dig my fingernails into the palm of my hand to stop myself from coming. All the while, we never took our eyes off the heaving, entwined bodies that we could see through the steam. They were grabbing at each other; hands clawing at buttocks and tits, wet, steamy flesh making sexy slapping noises as they writhed about on the slippery marble. At one point the black man knelt and in the steam we could see his magnificent erection in profile before he drove his cock into the white woman who screamed in ecstasy.

I lay on my back and Ben crouched over me, our heads turned to the right so that we didn't miss a second of the live porn show before our eyes. My pussy was so swollen that the tip of Ben's dick on my lips and clitoris was almost painful, but when he forced his cock inside my engorged hole, it was the sweetest sensation imaginable. I let myself be fucked hard, never taking my eyes off the others. As Ben pounded away, so ferociously that my whole body slid up the wooden bench, I made eye contact with the woman who was being fucked just yards away from me. Soon we were all looking at each other, six people but just two sets of bodies, all lost in what we were doing, what we were seeing and what was being done to us. The white guy opposite me looked at my tits with raw lust, even as he was fondling and squishing the breasts of the black girl. His animal desire was a huge aphrodisiac and the harder he stared, the more intensely I felt Ben's cock inside me. And I was really getting off on watching the other women; the more time I spent on this ship, the more obsessed I became with other women's tits. I loved watching them jiggle as they moved, I was fascinated by the way nipples changed shape, size and even colour as the women were turned on. No wonder men are so obsessed with breasts. One by one, the four people opposite us surrendered to their climaxes, faces blurred by the clouds of steam but their voices carrying perfectly. Their moans overlapped, giving a whole new meaning to multiple orgasm.

This was more than Ben could take; he came hard, much faster than he usually did. 'I'm sorry, baby,' Ben said, pulling his limp penis out of my cunt, a thread of his spunk trailing from the tip of his dick to my pussy like a spiderweb. 'It was just too horny for me. Come here,' he said, spreading my legs with his hand. 'I'll get you there.'

'Allow me,' said a high, smoky voice from somewhere in the mist. It was the woman with the blonde hair, the one I'd just seen being speared by the black guy's impressive hard-on. Now that she was close, I could see how horny she was. Her fair hair was tousled and wavy because of the steam, and her light golden tan was complimented by a blush on her cheeks and across her chest. But what I really liked was her dark, rose-gold nipples, which tipped her large, tear-shaped breasts.

'I'm thirsty,' she said, and before I could respond, she put her head between my legs and placed her lips on my pussy. I could feel her nipples rubbing my shins as she greedily sucked out Ben's sperm. I could feel the sensation inside my cunt like a little hoover. Briefly, the woman raised her face: her cheeks and lips were glazed with my natural juices and my lover's spunk. Ben was entranced; I could see him register every detail, storing it in his memory bank. We'd talk about this later, tell each other the story of the time the gorgeous blonde drank his cum from my pussy.

'I've had my fun,' she whispered. 'Now it's your turn.' And she was back between my legs, now giving my throbbing, twitching clitoris the attention it needed, her tongue expertly licking and sucking on it until the waves of orgasm rocked me from head to toe and hot liquid pleasure ran through my veins. After she'd finished licking me dry, she turned to Ben and sucked the oozing white tear off the end of his cock before licking her lips and crawling back to the lover she'd come in with.

Ben and I lay in the steam, unable to believe what had just happened.

'That,' said Ben eventually, 'Was the most intense thing that's ever happened to me.'

'Fuck, yeah,' I said. 'And we don't even know their names.'

We kissed, our sweaty bodies fusing together in the steam as the white mist engulfed us.

The next afternoon we were sunbathing naked on the roof terrace. Glistening bodies surrounded us and the sun's hot rays on our skin made us feel sexy and languid. We kissed, lazily, and stroked each other, Ben fingering my clitoris as I bounced his hard cock from one palm to the other. We alternated between fooling around like this and watching other couples, who were taking things further than we were right now. In the pool, a circle of people gathered round a woman who lay back on a lilo, fucking herself with her fist. On a balcony above the water, two women were taking it in turns to spank each other over their laps, the sharp slap of palms descending on to buttocks drawing attention to them.

I was rubbing sun lotion into Ben's erection when a young woman in a bunny-girl outfit presented us with a gilt-edged card on a silver tray.

'From the Captain,' she said, and stood above us while I opened the card and read it aloud.

'Alan and Suki invite you to dine with them at the Captain's Table this evening, followed by cocktails in the Captain's quarters. RSVP.' Ben and I looked at each other, eyes shining with excitement. We had been chosen by the Captain himself for one of his exclusive sex parties! We asked the bunny girl to convey our acceptance to the Captain and reached for each other, celebrating with a long, slow kiss.

That night, we dressed for dinner in the best clothes we had brought with us. Ben wore a fitted grey T-shirt with a black designer suit he'd splashed out on for this trip. The trousers showed off the gorgeous swell of his arse and his long, lean legs. I wore a gold lamé dress with a neckline slashed to the navel and a hemline slashed to the thigh.

We arrived at the Captain's Table at 8 p.m. to find it set for not four, but six people. We were thrilled to find that as well as Adam and Suki we would be dining with the red-haired woman and her handsome, dark lover. I was so excited to be seated next to such beautiful, sexy individuals that I could barely touch my food.

The red-haired girl was introduced as Maya and the dark-haired man with the turquoise eyes extended a hand and said, 'Hi, I'm Greg. Good to meet you guys. Are you English, too?'

Shaking hands with Greg, I knew instantly that there was chemistry there. His flesh sizzled on mine. I saw Maya look approvingly at Ben's chest and strong arms, and felt a surge of pride and excitement. We chatted; polite small talk at first which grew flirtier, dirtier and more intense as the night wore on. Maya and I had a lot in common, but even though she was a fascinating, intelligent woman, I found it hard to concentrate on what she was saying. She was so extraordinary-looking, green almond-shaped eyes in a cat-like face, pale skin with a smattering of freckles on her cheekbones and that luscious red hair that tumbled down her back, caressing my arm sensually whenever she leaned in to make a point. I couldn't help but wonder what colour her nipples were; I imagined they would be pale pink. Would her bush match her flaming hair and eyebrows? And would her pussy lips be pink, red or brown?

While I was talking to Greg and Maya, Ben was deep in conversation with Adam and Suki. When Suki placed her hand on Ben's crotch, I felt a thrill of anticipation: the first move had been made. After that, everything happened very naturally. Adam, who sat on the other side of Maya, began to stroke her long, Titian hair. Maya extended her own hand and placed it just under one of my breasts, a gesture so arousing that my nipple instantly hardened and swelled, protruding proudly through the gold lamé of my dress. I looked over and saw that Greg was tracing one finger along Suki's collarbone and as I watched, her head darted down, she took his finger in her mouth and sucked it gently, letting him probe her full, glossy lips. He closed his eyes and moaned. Greg's dick began to stiffen and swell. Unable to stop myself, I reached for it, placed my hand on the crotch of his trousers, felt the flesh beneath stir and expand under my fingers. The faster I fondled Greg, the harder Maya pinched my nipples, squeezing them between thumb and forefinger until I let out a whimper of helpless pleasure. When I moaned, her eyes lit up and she licked her pale pink lips. We were all

connected to each other, our bodies conducting an electric current of arousal that grew stronger with every second.
I was aware that many of the people in the main hall were
watching us as we touched each other and I felt the first
warm wetness seep out of my slit.

Adam cleared his throat. 'This is the point at which
I usually suggest we retire to my quarters for cocktails,'
he said, giving me a wink.

All eyes in the banqueting hall were on us as we left
the table and filed, one by one, through a door marked
PRIVATE that in turn led down a short, red-walled
corridor to a large oak door. The door led to a suite of
rooms that far outshone our own. Huge picture windows
opened on to a secluded balcony, affording us a view of
the flat sea and the starry sky. The main room was dominated by a bed two or three times the size of the one in
our cabin. A glass shelf displayed a range of designer sex
toys made of Perspex and chrome, a clear liquid that
looked like lube was housed in a crystal decanter and
bowls of different kinds of condoms were arranged on
every surface.

Wild now with desire and anticipation, a little more
juice oozed from between my legs. I could smell the natural
musk that meant I was really, really horny and wondered
if anyone else could smell me, too – and if it was turning
them on. My body was thrumming with sexual energy

and I felt that the slightest touch from any one of these new people could have had me coming hard right then. I needed to feel strange hands on my body, I needed Ben to watch me be rammed by another man's cock, and most of all, I needed to know what it felt like to take another woman's tit in my mouth.

Adam and Suki took the lead. He began to undress her, unfastening the halter-tie of her blue dress and exposing her high, small, firm breasts for all of us to see.

'Gentlemen,' he said. 'If we could all unveil our ladies.' At his command, Greg turned to Maya and dropped to his knees, his strong hands lifting the hem of her floaty white dress and pushing the billowing fabric as he rose up, sending it upwards in a white cloud that gradually revealed her porcelain skin. Her bush was the same fiery red as her hair, and her breasts were full and pendulous with nipples so pale pink that they almost blended into the rest of her skintone. As Maya locked eyes with me, I saw them harden and darken and my own nipples responded in kind.

Meanwhile Ben was tugging at the gold spaghetti straps that held my own dress together, yanking the skin-tight garment down the length of my body. I saw that all eyes were on me as Ben whipped the dress away, and I felt as if I were an exotic piece of fruit that was being peeled, ready to be eaten.

When she was naked but for her jewelled sandals, Suki turned to Adam and began to disrobe him. I watched as she undid his white tailored uniform jacket and slid it from his shoulders, carefully placing it on the back of his chair. She'd clearly performed this routine a million times before but when she gazed at Adam's broad, muscular chest, she did it with the awestruck lust of a woman seeing her lover's body for the first time. She removed his trousers with the same practised elegance, leaving Adam naked but for his hat. His smooth, dark-pink dick was beginning to stand to attention. Suki stepped up close to him, parted her legs and put the tip of his penis between her slender brown thighs, and squeezed. Adam let out a moan of pleasure, and the two of them kissed deeply.

Following Suki's lead, Maya and I both began to strip our men, although not with quite the same smooth manoeuvres. Rather, our efforts involved shoes being kicked off, clothes tugged and torn, straining hard-ons eagerly released from boxer shorts and kisses snatched while buttons flew off shirts. Ben's dick looked as good as I'd ever seen it. I was as wet as he was hard, and he was very, very hard. I made my hand into a loose fist and he thrust his dick into my palm, breathing deeply as I squeezed the round, sensitive tip of his cock. Maya looked similarly proud of Greg's dick, and with good reason: it was long and pink and stood upright, bouncing in anticipation of whatever was going to happen next.

Adam took Suki by the hand and led her to the vast bed. Sitting on the side of the bed her small, peachy arse making a tiny indentation on the smooth, scarlet silk, Suki extended one dainty foot up towards her husband. Tenderly he unfastened her jewelled shoe and placed it on the floor, then repeated the process with her other foot. Suki raised both legs straight out in front of her and pressed the soles of her feet on either side of Adam's bulging cock. As she stimulated him with subtle squeezes of her feet, his dick grew bigger and harder. When he could take no more, Suki whipped her feet away, revealing the shiny purple tip of Adam's twitching dick. Suki rolled over to the middle of the bed and spread her legs so that we could all see her pussy. It was a dark, plump and wet, like an oyster glistening in its shell. Adam followed his wife on to the bed and they embraced, rolling over so that she was on top of him, her honeyed body making slow, sensual motions on top of his pale, solid form. She arched her back, tossed her sleek hair over one shoulder and looked at Ben and me, and at Greg and Maya.

'Would you like to come and join us?' she asked. There was nothing I wanted more. Ben and I approached the vast bed from the right-hand side while Maya and Greg approached from the left. All six of us were on the bed now.

I mounted Ben but didn't let him penetrate me, instead I copied Suki's example and squeezed his dick between my clenched thighs, enjoying the way the base of his penis rubbed against my clit. Ben yelped in pleasure and frustration. I looked down at his face and we shared a secret smile, neither of us able to believe that this was really happening. I was inches away from Adam and Suki, who were still locked in their embrace. I could hear her every sigh and see each individual hair on his arms and chest.

On the other side of the Captain and his wife, Greg and Maya were moving together, his body on top of hers. I saw the muscles in his back ripple as he propped himself up on his forearms and bent his head to Maya's breast. I watched in frustrated fascination as his lips closed over her tit, as the nipple disappeared and then the surrounding flesh was sucked up by Greg's voracious mouth. Again, I wondered what that would feel like, how it would be to have Maya's tits in my mouth. Thinking about it made me wetter still and I dipped my finger into my pussy, held it to Ben's nose so he would know just how turned on I was. I closed my eyes, imagined being penetrated by Ben's cock while Maya stuffed her breasts in my face, suffocated me with the soft white pillows of her flesh.

At that point Adam's hand reached out to my own breast, grabbed hold of one of my swollen, sensitive nipples and pulled down hard. 'You,' he said, his face darkening with desire, 'I want you to come with me.' I looked at Ben and he nodded, taking his dick in his hands, stroking himself frantically at the thought of seeing Adam fuck me. Aggressively, Adam pulled me away from Ben and down towards him, holding me by the neck as he kissed me, his lips and tongue voraciously exploring the contours of my mouth.

Suki rolled off Adam and made a similar grab for Greg, whispering something in his ear that I couldn't quite catch. Whatever it was made him close his eyes and moan with pleasure. Maya's lips parted, her whole body quivering with excitement as she watched Greg lock lips with Suki and share a long, lingering kiss.

Behind me, I sensed Ben crawl across the bed towards Maya. I heard the soft slap of skin on skin as their bodies collided, and the thud as they fell together on to the bed.

Now I was with Adam, Ben was with Maya, and Greg was with Suki and all of us were lost in exploring new bodies for the first time. Adam was harder, more muscular than Ben, and his kisses and caresses were rougher and more urgent than I was used to. The raw, animal nature of his desire awakened the same in me and I clawed at his flesh, rubbed my clit against the tip of his penis, let the kisses that I planted on his lips turn into savage little nips and bites.

After a few moments of urgent, passionate kissing,

Adam broke away and pulled three condoms out of a bowl by the bed, handing one to Ben and one to Greg. Kneeling, he rolled a sheath on to his own dick, smoothing it down with a practised hand. I crouched on all fours, feeling my pussy flutter as I watched the orgy around me in full swing.

Greg lay on his back while Suki used her mouth to put a condom over his hard-on. Then, facing away from him, she squatted over his dick and lowered herself down on to him. As his dick disappeared into the folds of her body, they both moaned in ecstasy. Slowly, Suki leaned back and extended her legs so that she was lying on her back, on top of Greg. His arms reached around her body where he began massaging and kneading her tiny triangular tits with one hand, pulling her pussy lips apart with the other and frantically fingering her clitoris. The base of his dick was just visible as he thrust in and out of her. I watched them, fascinated, envious, horny as hell.

Maya was on all fours opposite me, close enough to reach out and touch. Behind her, Ben stroked his huge hard-on one last time before swiftly rolling a condom on to it. Then, with a forcefulness I found wildly arousing, he pulled a long, twisting lock of her red hair and yanked her head back, forcing her body to buck. Maya's eyes turned glassy and she began to breathe deeply, a soft pink blush spreading across her bouncing, swinging tits, as she let Ben slide into her. Still holding her hair, he rode her like a pony, thrusting his dick all the way into her, pulling it out, spearing her white flesh again, in and out, in and out.

I felt hands on my own tits then as Adam grabbed me by both breasts and propelled his cock into me with such merciless force that I screamed. The relief of finally being penetrated was overwhelming and I succumbed to Adam's will, letting him pull and pinch my tits, enjoying his fat cock pumping hard in my pussy.

Opposite me, Maya was being fucked by Ben and looked as ecstatic as I was. And to my side, Suki writhed about on top of Greg, eyes closed, lost in her own pleasure. Maya and I locked eyes, sharing a secret smile at the intensity of the moment. Her milky tits were swinging to and fro, slapping against each other and against her ribs. I was hypnotised by the pale, pendulous breasts and even as I watched them, I saw Suki's small, dark hand reach up and close over one of Maya's breasts, squeezing hard so that the flesh spilled out between bony fingers. Then Suki grabbed my breast, did the same thing. I felt my pussy twitch and flutter: I was ready to come. All it would take would be the tiniest pressure on my clitoris. Inwardly I prayed for Suki to touch me there, to allow me my orgasm, to give me the release I craved so badly.

'You know what I'd like to see?' Suki's high, clear voice

cut through the collective moaning and groaning. 'I'd like to see Maya and Charmaine together. You're both so sexy,' she said to us. 'I'd love to see that. Nothing would get me wetter than seeing that.'

My heart started to pound. Have Maya all to myself while everyone watched? I was so aroused I couldn't speak, couldn't do anything more than nod my consent. Ben, Adam and Greg all murmured their approval. Adam removed his dick from my twitching pussy, Ben pulled out of Maya and Greg released Suki from his arms and winced as she rolled off his bloated dick. Suki pulled the condoms off each man in turn.

'And while the girls are fucking,' she said in a kittenish voice, 'I want you boys to come all over me. Decorate me. I want you to write your names on my tits in spunk.' Obediently, Ben, Adam and Greg lined up before Suki and began tugging and stroking their dicks frantically, their eyes darting between me and Maya facing each other on the bed and Suki's lithe body outstretched before them.

Maya and I knelt opposite each other. Tentatively, I reached for her, pressed my lips against hers. She kissed me back, slowly at first and then more passionately, her soft, velvety lips sucking my face, her pink tongue darting in and out of my mouth, duelling with my own tongue and tracing my teeth. She wrapped her arms around my neck, drew me in closer and took her lips away from mine, whispering words that caused hot droplets of moisture to ooze from between my legs and dampen my bush.

'I know you want to suck my tits,' she said. 'I need it too. Go on. Do it.' I didn't need to be told twice; I picked up her tear-shaped tit and pressed it to my lips. Suckling on her nipple was heavenly but stuffing the rest of her breast in my mouth was almost enough to make me come on its own. I was aware of the guys voicing their appreciation and of Maya's high-pitched wails of pleasure. I felt her nipple on the roof of my mouth, forced it even further back into my throat, used my tongue to stimulate the fleshy underside of her breast until at last I had to come up for air.

She pulled me in close, kissed me again, and this time I was aware of our two pussies rubbing together and the clash and friction of her tits, one still damp with my saliva, rasping against mine. I felt her slender fingers walk down the side of my body and then gently comb out my bush before she placed her fingers on my clitoris. As soon as she touched me there I began to shake uncontrollably, and instinctively I reached for her pussy, too. She was as wet as I was: both of us frantically rubbed each other's dripping, eager clits, harder and harder, while the guys wanked faster and faster and Suki lay on the bed, wriggling like a little eel, fucking herself with a sex toy and screaming orders.

'Come in my face!' she was begging. 'Come on my tits. Come on my arse!'

Greg was the first to obey her, shooting a thick white stream of spunk on to Suki's tits. Ben followed seconds later, his juice squirting into her open mouth and decorating her neck. Finally Adam directed a hot jet on to her pussy and clitoris: it was this final sensation that sent Suki over the edge, and Maya and I stopped fondling each other for a few seconds to watch Suki's spectacular orgasm: she writhed, gripped the bed and a puddle of liquid seeped out of her pussy to stain the sheets. As soon as she had calmed down, all three men advanced on Suki, rubbing their mixed juices into her skin as though they were massaging a princess.

Maya and I turned our attention back to each other. 'I'm so near coming,' I said. 'You've made me so fucking horny.' I took her lower lip between my teeth and resumed my frantic stroking of her clitoris while she reached for mine with trembling hands. I felt an unmistakable heat suffuse my body and then my orgasm came, crashing over me at the same time as Maya's body gave a violent shudder. I bit down on her lip even harder, breathed in the scream of pleasure that she let out, softened my kiss as we both held each other, letting the aftershocks of our simultaneous climaxes shudder through our bodies.

All six of us, now spent, sank into a sweaty tangled

heap, limbs entwined, eyes closed. Occasionally a hand I couldn't identify would trail a feathery caress along my skin, and I would reach out and touch someone else in a similar way. We remained there, talking and touching, until Adam and Suki announced that the evening was over.

'Thank you so much for coming,' said Suki as we all dressed. 'You've been the best guests we've ever had.' She ushered Ben and me, and Greg and Maya out into the corridor to go our separate ways. We said goodbye to Maya and Greg; he leaned in and kissed me, a tender kiss goodbye, while Maya tongued Ben and gave his arse a playful squeeze. Then, unexpectedly, she pulled me to her and pressed her lips against mine, that long tongue sweeping around my mouth while she pushed her pubic bone into my body, an echo of the embrace we'd shared just moments before. It provoked a searing heat between my legs that made my body pulse and quiver again, eager for more. I think if she'd stayed kissing me I would have been ready to fuck her all over again, but she drew away. 'And you,' she murmured into my ear. 'I want to see you again tomorrow. We can party in our cabin. What do you think?' I nodded, thrilled that Ben and I would enjoy a private party with this amazing couple again the next night. And that this time, we wouldn't have to share them with Adam and Suki.

When we finally got back to our own cabin, we saw

the dawn break over the calm water through our window. Utterly exhausted and satisfied beyond any experience, I curled up in my naked lover's arms and smiled as I drifted off to sleep.

SHOPPED

❦

I'm always fascinated by women who take crazy risks just for the hell of it. Like Nicole. She's a professional woman who gets her kicks shoplifting things she doesn't really need from exclusive department stores. This is the story of the day she took one risk too many – and found herself in a situation far beyond her control. Enjoy.

I love beautiful things. Clothes, make-up, jewellery. Sometimes, I even pay for them. But my favourite trinkets – the ones I treasure most of all – are the ones I get by stealth, not wealth. I'm an expert shoplifter. I've been doing it for years. I can outsmart the CCTV systems in most major department stores. It's not just about getting something for nothing; I'm addicted to the risk. I live for the thrill I get when I march out of those doors, past those big burly security guards with a twenty-quid lipstick tucked in my sleeve. The more guards or the more cameras that are trained on me, the bigger the buzz when I get away with it. And when I walk out into the street, the release of tension and the blood soaring in my ears and oh, it's the nearest thing you can get to having an orgasm. I'm a danger junkie, I'm crazy, I know. But I'm good at it. I've only been caught once.

Oh yes, the time I got caught. I was in my favourite haunt, an old department store in the middle of town. It's an impressive building, with an interior dominated by a gilt spiral staircase. The luxurious beauty hall stocks face creams that cost a day's paypacket for some people, often more.

I browsed the store for a while, looking for something to take my fancy. In the end, I chose a sleek designer lippie. I even tried it out in the mirror before I committed myself to stealing it. It was a lovely colour, rose pink with a soft sheen. Even under the shop counter's harsh lighting, I could tell that it turned my average pair of lips into a pair of petals, plump and velvety. And so the second the salesgirl turned around to talk to another customer, I slid it up the top of my sleeve with a sleight of hand that would put most TV magicians to shame.

As I made my way to the huge double doors my heart was pounding, the way it does when you're about to kiss someone for the first time. The metallic casing of the lipstick was clinically cold against the hot, fast pulse that raced on the inside of my wrist. I raised my hand to push the heavy door open.

And that's when I felt it. The hand on the shoulder. My blood ran cold. It sounds crazy, but I had never prepared myself for this eventuality. I didn't believe I'd ever actually get caught. I froze. I couldn't see the hand but I felt a presence, a huge bulk of a man towering behind me. A man this big would be strong, too. No point in trying to run. It would only make things worse for me.

I turned around slowly, got ready to flutter my eyelashes at the security guard, hoping that I could flirt my way out of it. I found myself eye-level with his chest, a great solid wall of upper body. A blue shirt strained to contain a vast torso, short sleeves displayed strong, wide arms dusted with thick, dark hair. And above the collar, a stern, unsmiling face that didn't look like it was about to be melted by my little-girl-lost act.

'Madam, would you like to come with me?' he said in a rough, gravelly voice. He phrased it as a question but there was no doubt that it was an order. He placed his hand lightly on my arm, not quite restraining me. His thick fingers could probably crush my arm if he wanted. I had no choice but to follow as he led me through a side door (why had I never noticed it before? Usually too focused on a successful getaway, I guess) and up a narrow steel staircase.

'Where are we going?' I said, and then, to cover myself, 'I don't know what I'm supposed to have done.'

He stayed silent, conserving his breath as we mounted the steep flight of stairs. I had to catch my breath but my gasps were barely audible above the pounding of my heart in my ears. I felt scared and guilty and angry with myself but the adrenaline junkie in me was also rather excited. Finally, I was experiencing something even more thrilling and shocking than the act of stealing itself.

The guard maintained his silence as he unlocked a wooden door and led me into a tiny room. He locked the door behind him, putting the key in his pocket, effectively making me his prisoner. I looked around the cell-sized room. There was a desk, a chair and about thirty TV screens, each showing a different part of the store. There was also a tiny window at about eye level from which you could see the entire shop floor. I was astonished. With CCTV this good, I was surprised they hadn't caught me months ago. I was so surprised that I forgot to be frightened.

'Oh look!' I said brightly. 'You can see the make-up counter from here!'

I turned around, but he wasn't smiling. The room was so small that there wasn't much space between us. Close up, I could detect a clean, soapy smell that masked an undertone of something more dark, feral and masculine. I noticed that he hadn't shaved for a few days, and that there was a small scar on his chin which made a bare patch in the stubble. I've always found men with scars irresistible. They make a man look tough and powerful – which, by contrast, makes me feel vulnerable and ultra-feminine. In other circumstances, I'd have found this guy extremely attractive.

'I've got something else to show you,' he said, hazel eyes stern beneath a furrowed brow, and he slid a tape into a VCR machine. At first, it was nothing special – just a series of shots of the shop interior. Then I saw someone I recognised: dark hair and a black leather jacket, suspiciously large red handbag – oh God, it was me!

I watched in horror as the camera captured me sliding a blue g-string and matching bra into my bag. Then the video cut to another film, another day – hotter, because I wore no jacket, but I had the same oversized bag. This time I watched myself casually drop a forty-pound bottle of shampoo into my bag before leaving via the main doors. Then another film of me stealing a clingy white dress. And another, showing me taking some expensive perfume. And another. And another. All the little crimes I thought I'd got away with had been taped. He had enough evidence here to put me in prison. This wasn't going to be just a little slap on the wrist. My job – my flat – my life – suddenly I realised quite how much I'd put in jeopardy to feed my habit for cheap thrills.

'I don't understand,' I said, and this time when I looked at him the tears brimming in my eyes were real. 'Why have you been holding on to all this? What are you going to do with it? Why arrest me today?'

'Today was different,' he said, matter-of-factly. 'I like the way your tits look in that top, so I thought, today will be the day that I fuck her.'

'What?' I stammered. I stood there for a second, unsure that I'd heard right but I knew I had.

'I've been watching you for months,' he said, moving closer to me. I took a step back but there was nowhere to go. My back was against the door as he continued speaking. 'The first time I saw you, I thought, she's a cheeky little bitch, that one, she's arrogant, thinks she'll never get caught. But then you bent down to look at something, and I got a look at your arse in your tight jeans, and I thought, I'd rather fuck her than nick her. I knew you'd be back. I've come across your type before. Posh girls like you, stealing for kicks always think you can get away with it. So I waited. And I recorded you. Every time I see you coming in I get hard, thinking about how one day I'm going to take you up here and what I'm going to do to you.'

I stood mute, my body trembling.

'Now,' he said, waving the tape under my nose. 'I've got enough evidence here to send you to prison for a fair few months. I reckon you've stolen at least five grand's worth of stuff from this shop in the last year.' He smiled a humourless smile revealing white teeth, and pointed to a sign on the wall that read: WE ALWAYS PROSE-CUTE THIEVES. 'So I've got a deal to make with you. You drop your stolen knickers for me here, and I'll destroy the tape in front of you.'

'And if I don't?' I asked.

'And if you don't, then you're going to wish you'd never set foot in this shop, princess, because your nice little life will be *ruined*.'

My mind raced; all the things I had to lose flashed before me. I wished I'd never shoplifted in the first place, but it was too late for pointless regrets like that now. And then I conjured another series of mental images, of me on the desk being screwed by this evil giant fucker of a security guard. It didn't turn me on, but it didn't repulse me either. I swallowed, and decided to take the cock. The only problem, I thought, looking at his broad chest and thick fingers again, was the size of him. I'd always had slim, athletic lovers in the past. If this guy's dick was in proportion to the rest of him, how would I get wet enough to accommodate him?

'Whatever you want,' I said, looking at the floor.

'Good girl,' said the guard, smiling again. 'Right,' he said. 'We haven't got long. I'm back on duty in ten minutes.

So to keep this quick and efficient, and to keep your end of the bargain, I'll be in charge here. You'll do exactly what I say.'

I nodded meekly, just wanting it over now that I'd agreed to do it.

'Take your clothes off then,' he said. With trembling hands, I began to undo my button-through dress, taking as long as possible to delay the inevitable until I realised that he might think I was indulging him in a striptease. It was anything but! I hung the dress on the back of the door and bent down to undo the straps of my shoes. Now I was before him in only my underwear: the blue bra and panties set that I had just watched myself steal on video. His hand slid to his crotch where he started stroking himself, but he stayed fully clothed.

'Keep going,' he said, with a leer. Slowly, I removed my panties, hooking my thumbs under the waistband before sliding them down my legs. I took my bra off and my tits stood up pert, nipples hard in the chill of the air-conditioned room.

'Lie back on the desk,' he commanded. I did so, the hard plastic surface freezing cold under my skin. I yelped in discomfort.

'Spread your legs,' he said. He put his face between my legs, his warm breath caressing my pussy lips. To my surprise, I felt pleasant stirrings at the stimulation. He examined me for a second or two, then placed a thumb on my pussy.

'You're not wet enough to take me yet,' he said, disapprovingly. 'Do something about that.'

'What?' I said.

'Get yourself ready for me.' He stood back, arms folded, and waited. I had no choice but to bring my hand down between my legs. With one finger either side of my clitoris, I began rubbing myself the way I always do when I want to get off. It was a tried and tested masturbation technique which had never failed me yet. But then, I'd never had to do it to order before. I'd always been horny before I started playing with myself in the past.

Doing it now, under this man's instructions, was weird. I was dry down there, which made the friction uncomfortable, so I slid my finger into my pussy to use some of my own juices as a natural lubricant. I closed my eyes, tried to lose myself in fantasy, but then the guard barked, 'Keep your eyes open, you little bitch. I want you to look at me, think about what you've done.'

I locked eyes with him, and we were staring each other out as my body started to respond. I felt the first warm drops of moisture start to flow into my pussy as the whole area began to grow warm and tingle. Relief mingled with pleasure flooded my body. I wasn't exactly going to come, but I would be wet enough to take his cock.

He put his face down there again and examined me. I was getting really horny now: I craved his tongue against my clit, wanted the harsh stubble on his cheeks to scrape the skin on my thighs.

'Okay, you're ready,' he said, as though I were a joint of meat and he was considering whether it was time to carve and serve me. 'You're ready for cock. Now you need to get me ready. Off the desk and on to your knees. Now! And don't you fucking dare close your eyes again. Hear me?'

I nodded, and clambered awkwardly down from the desk and sank to my knees. I heard the wet noise of him licking his lips in anticipation and then the unmistakable sound of a belt buckle, then a zipper, being unfastened. I looked up at him as instructed and found myself in front of the biggest dick I had ever seen in my life. It was the size of a baby's arm, and getting bigger by the second. My eyes bulged in disbelief and fear as it grew more upright, thicker and harder. Veins pulsed along the side of it.

'I've been getting hard for you for months now,' he said, a note of cruelty in his voice. 'But I could do with being a little bit harder. What do you think?'

Before I could reply he thrust the tip of his cock between my lips, forcing them wide open. As the first few inches of his dick penetrated my mouth, I knew it was going to be too much. He probed harder into me. I tried to scream but the noise was muffled. I gagged as he rammed my face, trying to stuff a huge dick into a space not big enough to accommodate it.

'You never thought this would be the consequence of your actions, did you?' he snarled as he fucked my throat, harder and harder. 'You never thought you'd end up on your knees in here, did you? Never thought about *this*?' Just when I thought I couldn't take any more he pulled out and used his dick to slap first one cheek, then the other. I fell on all fours, gasping for breath. He yanked up my hair so that I was level with him again, and before I could say no, he was there, in my mouth again. And to my surprise, this time around, I found that my pussy was throbbing and my subconscious voiced an animal desire that had suddenly risen up in me: 'I wish he was fucking me in the pussy and not my face.' As soon as I had spoken the words to myself, I felt a rush of heat to my cunt. I was ready to take him inside me. I *needed* to take him inside me.

'Okay,' he said, and pulled me to my feet again. By now I was so turned on that my whole body had become liquid and my legs could barely support my weight. I was eye level with his chest, his huge dick banging against the skin on my navel.

'Back on the desk,' he growled. Somehow, I managed

to climb back up there, lay on my back, and spread my legs to expose my quivering, waiting, hungry hole.

'Okay, you're gonna get it,' he said hovering over me. He took a deep breath and thrusted. The tip of his dick was soft and round against the wet lips of my pussy. Moments later, I felt a searing pain as he drove his huge rod into me. It felt like I would split in two. Pain turned to pleasure within a second. The harder he pumped my pussy, the wetter it got and soon he was sliding that great big truncheon in and out of me so fast and I couldn't have enough of it. I felt my nipples start to harden and stiffen. He lightly slapped my tits. I whimpered with pleasure.

'Oooh,' he said, and now it was his voice that was unsteady. 'She's getting into it now. She's enjoying her punishment. She wants it harder,' and with that he speared me really viciously. I had to grab on to the sides of the desk to stop his violent thrusts propelling me off the edge. His face grew darker and as it suffused with blood, that scar on his chin, that horny, bad-boy scar, grew more pronounced.

'She wants more,' he said, and I wasn't even sure that he was talking to me any longer or himself. 'She can take a little more.' And with that he brought his hand down in a hard slap on my clitoris. The sudden, intense stimulation made me yell out with pleasure.

'She deserves everything she gets,' he said, raining down tiny slaps on my clit. I felt myself begin to lose control. As he fucked my pussy and spanked my clit relentlessly my whole body went limp for a few seconds before I came, violent spasms and a trickle of my fluids grabbing his hard-on in a warm, wet caress.

'Oh yeah,' he murmured, whipping his dick out of my still-spasming pussy and at the last moment forcing it between my lips. He shot his load into my mouth. I swallowed, aware that a sliver of hot, salty liquid was spilling between my lips and rolling down my neck.

Immediately after he'd come, he wiped himself with a tissue, put his dick back in his trousers, and looked at the clock. When I swivelled my body around and sat up on the desk, my pounded pussy was so sore I couldn't put my legs together. He noticed and gave a cruel, bitter laugh.

'You won't be able to walk properly again for days,' he said. 'It will be a constant reminder of your punishment. And I let you off lightly for what you did, you spoilt little bitch.' Wordlessly, he handed me the tape, allowed me a few seconds to clothe myself. I didn't even have time to wipe myself clean of the trickle of semen that was beginning to dry on my neck. He led me out of the tiny little room, down a side staircase before pushing me out of a fire door and into the sunny street, where I stood blinking in disbelief for a few seconds, still coming down from the high of my orgasm.

I hopped on the bus, eager to get home so I could

fantasise about the whole experience again. By the time I got back to my flat, I was planning what I could shoplift next time. It would have to be something daring and outrageous, something that would guarantee a repeat performance. Like I said, I'm a danger junkie.

FIREMAN'S POLE

Jules didn't want to share this confession with me. It's the story of how she had one final fling before her wedding, and it was very out of character. Jules, you see, is a good girl. That's how she thought of herself. She'd always been faithful to her fiancé. Always done the right thing by her friends. But sometimes even good girls succumb to temptation. And when they do, the results are often intensely orgasmic.

The last thing I said to Fiona before my hen night was, 'I don't want a stripper. Please don't get me a stripper.' I'd seen too many brides-to-be have their big night ruined as they cringed while some banana-and-whipped-cream-wielding moron who fancies himself and is covered in fake tan sticks a leopard print thong in her face. 'I don't mind the L-plates or the badges and all that stuff, but I'd be so embarrassed by a stripper. Do you promise?'

'Would I do that to you, Jules?' said Fiona with a wicked grin. She was my oldest friend, and the only contender for chief bridesmaid. She was a great mate and a fantastic organiser. She'd booked a meal in a fancy West End restaurant and then got us VIP tickets for an exclusive club. But she also had a wicked sense of humour and a taste for the outrageous. On this occasion, Fiona's promise didn't mean much.

On the night itself, I dressed in a petrol-blue baby-doll dress that matched the colour of my eyes and the sapphire in my engagement ring. It also showed far too much cleavage and thigh, but I'd been working out for my wedding, and I wanted to show my newly buff body off.

'You look gorgeous,' said Danny, my fiancé, as I twirled before the mirror while I waited for my cab. 'A bit too gorgeous! I hope you'll stop dressing like that once you're a wife. This is your last big night. Don't go talking to any strange men, now.'

'Please,' I giggled, as he pulled me into his arms, stroked my long brown hair which fell in waves over my shoulders. 'It's a gang of twenty drunken women. We'll be scaring men off, not attracting them!'

'You have a good time, babe,' said Danny, and gave me a long, lingering kiss which was only interrupted by the honk of the taxi's horn. Fiona was in the cab, dressed to kill in a plunging pink dress that left little to the imagination.

'You might be getting married but I'm still looking for Mr Right!' she giggled. We sped through the London streets before finding ourselves in the private room of a fashionable restaurant. When I stepped foot inside, my eyes swam with tears of joy; all my closest female friends and family were gathered around the table. As I entered they rose to their feet and clapped and whistled. They'd decorated the room with pink feather boas and pictures of me on various girly holidays.

The night flew by. We ate a three-course dinner and drank our own weight in champagne. We posed for photographs and flirted with the very attractive waiters. After dinner, Fiona produced a bottle of sambuca and twenty shot glasses.

'Just a little something to awaken the palate after that wonderful supper,' she said pouring the clear liquid into the glasses and spilling half of it on to the silver tray. 'Now, the best way to drink this,' she continued, brandishing a silver Zippo lighter, 'is on fire.' And with that, she shot out a tiny flame across the surface of one of the glasses. An ethereal blue-purple flame danced over the top of the oily liquid. To my amazement, Fiona tipped the whole thing back and downed the shot in one.

'Now it's your turn!' she said to the rest of us. My hand shaking, I tipped the shot down my throat. The flame skimmed my lips, a fiery smack that awoke a distant memory somewhere in me, reminded me of the urgent kisses you only have with a new lover. I'd never have that 'first kiss' intensity again, I thought, as the hot liqueur flowed through my body, making my limbs tingle and my head swim.

Fiona poured another round of drinks and set them aflame. As I raised my glass, my friends fell silent and then began to giggle, staring behind me. Before I had a chance to turn around, a deep, masculine voice from behind me boomed, 'Do you need someone to put out a fire?'

I whipped around to see a tall, broad man in full fireman's uniform, complete with yellow helmet and visor, carrying a hose in one hand. Fiona produced a CD player seemingly from nowhere and music filled the room.

'Happy hen night, Jules!' said the fireman, whose face was still obscured by his headgear. He looked tall and well built, but really, in those bulky clothes and that hat, he could have been gorgeous or hideous underneath.

'You *bitch*,' I hissed at Fiona. She winked at me, and danced out of my way.

'Madam,' said the stripper, 'That drink breaks health and safety regulations. I'm going to have to extinguish it.' Too shocked to disobey, I sat down on a chair and let him take the drink from my hand and down it in one.

'Hey, that was mine!' I said, making everyone laugh. The ice broken, I decided to make the best of an awkward situation and enjoy my strippogram with good grace and a sense of humour.

He stood across me, broad legs straddling my body, his crotch and inch or two away from my mouth. He smelled freshly scrubbed but the faintest traces of his own natural aroma also caught my nostrils as I inhaled. It was literally years since I had been this close to any man but Danny; I had forgotten how overpowering and arousing a new man's smell can be.

I closed my eyes to drink in his scent, and when I opened them I found that he was sliding off his jacket. twenty young women gasped in admiration and arousal as he revealed a strong, broad torso with a perfect six-pack and not an inch of fat. His skin was a nutty light brown colour, and was perfectly smooth except for a curly line of hair that scurried down from his navel to beneath his waistband, and a similar smattering beneath his underarms. Dark brown nipples topped tight pecs, but the most beautiful part of his body was his arms. They were broad and muscular, worked-out arms, veins running along the length of them. He produced a tiny bottle of chocolate body paint from his pocket and drizzled it across his chest. Entranced, and playing the dutiful hen, of course, I put my lips to his nipples and licked the sweet chocolate liquid from his sweet chocolate skin. I stopped just above his waistband, but realised with shock that I wanted it to continue. A flush crept on to my cheeks at the same time as a faint pulse began to throb between my legs. What had started as a joke was fast turning into genuine, disturbing, intense desire – the kind of desire that demands gratification.

I drew away, drank from a glass of water to calm myself down. I shook my head at Fiona, mouthed the words 'I'll get you for this' at her across the room. She beamed back at me, clearly enjoying the entertainment.

The trousers were next to be removed, leaving his body in one swift movement. I was now face-to-face with a pair of beautiful brown thighs and a red pouch, padded to give the impression of a dick bigger than anything that could ever exist in real life. He dangled his crotch near to my face and I could see the individual hairs on his thighs. I leant in towards them, ready to lick up the chocolate body paint on his lower abdomen.

He removed his helmet then, to reveal a young man's face framed by close-cropped curls. He had a full smile and twinkly eyes under a strong brow. Now that we were making eye contact, my bravado evaporated and I snatched my head back, suddenly shy.

The stripper would have none of it. Egged on by screaming girls, he took my hands and placed them on his washboard stomach, encouraged me to feel every perfectly defined inch of his body. He felt smooth, young and firm underneath my fingertips. My friends giggled and cheered me on, and I hoped that they didn't realise just how turned-on I was getting. Thank God they were there, I thought to myself as my hands clawed at the solid flesh of his buttocks. And thank God I was in public. If I found myself alone with this guy, there was a very real chance that I would want to take this further.

Suddenly the 'fireman' grabbed my hand held it over his pouch. I shrieked with surprise and delight. What I had assumed was padding was definitely 100 per cent human, warm, pulsating flesh. I pressed the palm of my hand against the shaft of his dick and felt it stir beneath my touch. I pictured his erection, huge and hard and all for me, envisaged his balls swelling with spunk to be shot into my face. It was a long time since I'd had fantasies like this about a complete stranger, but then it was a long time since I'd been so close to such a hot guy. I blushed underneath my make-up.

The song on the stereo drew to a close, signalling that my dance had come to an end.

'I think the emergency's over,' he said with a smile. 'But I'm afraid I must evacuate you from the building, just to be on the safe side,' he continued, and scooped me up over his shoulder in a fireman's lift, as effortlessly as though I were a rag doll. My tits were pressed against his muscular back, my arse was over his shoulder and my short skirt had ridden up even further so that I could feel his breath on the top of my thighs. My hair hung down in long ropes, trailing against the back of his knees. I wondered if he liked the way it felt, silky against his skin. I wondered if that fledgling erection was growing as my legs dangled across the front of his body.

He carried me out of the room and down the corridor, my friends laughing and taking photographs as we went. The blood rushed to my head as he kept walking, and the fluttering sensation between my legs was growing more intense, my desire becoming more insistent. He stopped at the end of the corridor. Then he sank to his knees, strong legs flexing as he gently put me down. It was all over, but my hardening nipples and the growing damp puddle in my panties wanted more.

'Well,' he said. 'Thanks for being such a good sport. It's a rare privilege to work with such a beautiful hen. You can go back to your friends now.'

It was now or never. 'Do I have to?' I said.

He saw that I was serious. 'No,' he replied. 'It's your hen night. It's your special night. You can do whatever you want to do.'

'What I want to do,' I murmured, taking a step towards him so that our bodies were pressed together, 'Is *you*.'

There was a door leading to a balcony behind him. He kicked it open and dragged me through. We found ourselves on a fire escape, iron stairs overlooking a deserted side street. I didn't think of Danny, didn't think of my friends down the corridor, didn't think of anything but the pulsating and the moisture between my legs as my clit expanded and grew more sensitive, waiting for his touch.

He began to undress me with the same swiftness he'd removed his own clothes, sliding the spaghetti straps first over one shoulder, then the other. My breasts fell out of the built-in bra. He bent his head to my breast and began to kiss it. I leaned back against the cool brick wall and let him peel the rest of my dress off me. I was naked but for my shoes and panties.

Without warning he hooked his hands under my thighs and lifted me up, not bothering to remove my panties but pulling them to one side.

'God, you're soaking,' he said, as his fingers made contact with the damp cotton. I wrapped my arms around his neck and crossed my ankles just above his arse. My breasts and belly brushed against his torso, my nipples rubbing against his. He fumbled with his pouch and released a quivering hard-on. I felt his dick rise up immediately; the soft, smooth tip of it gently poked and prodded my pussy lips. By tilting his hips a little, he angled his dick so that its tip touched my clitoris, jabbed softy against my hard little bud, made my pussy twitch and quiver like a hungry mouth.

'I can't wait,' I said, feeling that I would die if I didn't know what his dick felt like. 'I need you inside me now.'

With smooth brown fingers he parted my pussy lips and exposed my hole. His thick, fat dick was in me in seconds, stretching my cunt to its limit. I buried my head on his muscular chest, pushed down on his hard-on with all my bodyweight. His pelvic bone jutted out, the tight curls of his pubic hair tickling and teasing my clitoris, sending pre-orgasmic judders throughout my body.

He pushed up into me as I bore down on him. Our moans of pleasure were perfectly syncopated as we groaned like wild animals, both of us approaching orgasm. The sound of skin on skin echoed through the city night as my tits slapped against him, and his balls against his thighs and on my arse. I rubbed against him, harder, faster, not caring about anything but this moment. Just when I was on the verge of coming, he jabbed a finger up my arse, and it triggered the release of tension that I had been waiting for. Even as the first orgasmic waves washed over me, I pushed my fingers into his firm buttocks, greedy, wanting him deeper and deeper into me. My climax was more intense and longer than any I'd had before, a series of tiny explosions in my body. My pussy contracted time after time, massaging his dick inside me. He came right after I did, a wordless orgasm. We stayed there for a few seconds, both getting our breath back. When he placed me back on the iron steps, both of us found that our legs were shaking.

We smiled at each other, both satisfied, both knowing that what we'd shared had been a thrilling, delicious one-off. I disappeared into the ladies' room on unsteady legs. As I locked myself in the bathroom, I could hear the stripper telling my friends I'd just gone to clean the chocolate off my face and I'd be back in a minute. By the time I'd wiped myself clean and returned to my friends, he was gone.

Fiona gave me a hug when I came back into the room. If she suspected what I'd just done, she said nothing about it. 'Are you very cross with me?' she said. 'I'm sorry. I saw his picture on the website and I just couldn't resist.'

'No,' I said. 'I'm not cross.' And I wasn't. Quite the opposite. I'd never been so grateful to anyone in my life.